EPILOGUE OF AN EPITAPH

ST. MARIN'S COZY MYSTERY SERIES - BOOK 8

ACF BOOKENS

1

Most people think of my dad as a quiet but charismatic man, someone who is always there, solid, good, but not prone to big outbursts of laughter. And definitely not someone who would play pranks.

I, however, knew better. In the privacy of his own home or when with close friends, my dad had a wild and silly streak. Once, when I had friends at our house for a sleepover, Dad spent almost an hour making scratching sounds against the wall and then hiding when we went to look for him. By the time he finally revealed himself and the hand rake in his closet next door, my friends were convinced that there was a ghost in our house and were about to call their parents to go home. He loves telling that story, even now, thirty years later.

So when the gossip network of St. Marin's reached me, I knew my dad was up to something. The rumor was that he was having an affair with his friend Thomas, a sort of torrid affair. My dad would never cheat on my mom. He adored that woman, and "torrid" and "public" were not exactly my dad's style.

Still, truth has little place in gossip, and the rumor spread through town like word of Lu's food truck after church on Sunday. Everyone who knew my dad well, including all my closest friends and colleagues, blew off the rumor when it reached them, but customers in my bookstore, they were another story. As soon as they heard my last name was Beckett, their faces flashed with something like surprise and then embarrassment, and because I loved my dad and knew that the rumors were not true, I always played along. "What is it? Do you know my family?" I'd say with mock innocence.

Most of the customers would pat my hand or buy an extra book out of sympathy as if those actions would make up for the very fake but very scandalous choices my dad was making. I, however, felt completely justified in taking their sympathy and their money if they were going to be as gullible as to believe gossip.

I had heard about my dad's "affair" from my favorite customer, Galen. He had come in one day after running a few other errands, and the grin on his face was as wide as his ears. "Harvey, you will not believe what I just heard at the post office."

I was puzzled because Galen was not a gossiper. In fact, he prided himself on being someone who looked up the truth of everything on Facebook before he shared it, so the idea that he was going to pass along a rumor was confusing to me. "You heard something I need to know?"

"*Need* probably isn't the right word, but *want*, yes." Then he told me how the postmistress, Mrs. Riordan, had whispered that she was worried about me and my mom because she had seen some "inappropriate" letters from my dad and Thomas Garrison. "She said she felt it was her duty to find out the truth and so had opened a couple of them to be sure that what she suspected was true. *And it was*," Galen finished with a waggle of his eyebrows.

"She opened their mail?!" I said, stunned more by that fact

than by any sort of romantic farce my dad was putting on. "Isn't that illegal?"

"Very," Galen said. "I looked it up on our way over." He glanced over at Mac, his English Bulldog, who had already fallen asleep next to my dogs, Taco and Mayhem, in the shop window. "Apparently, it's a felony and can result in two to five years in jail. I imagine Mrs. Riordan would get the heavier penalty given that she works for the postal service."

I sighed. "I don't need her to go to jail, of course, but, seriously. Do you think she opens everyone's mail?"

Galen shrugged. "Given how nonchalantly she told me about her activities, I imagine so. She even showed me the hot plate and tea kettle she used to steam open the seals."

"Good glory. She is brazen." I rolled my eyes toward the ceiling. "Well, what did the letters say?" I figured if the news was out, I should probably know exactly what the rumor was . . . or at least what it had started as. By the time it spread through the town, I imagined my dad was going to be rumored to be a straight-up hooligan.

"Apparently, they were love notes, very elaborate ones with testaments of adoration and a fair dousing in cologne." Galen laughed.

"My dad doesn't even wear cologne unless it is Old Spice aftershave. He is definitely playing at something." I was already reaching for my phone to call my dad and find out what was going on. "I'm getting the whole story, Galen. Find you with an update in a few?"

Galen said, "Please," and headed off to the mystery section for his weekly stack of cozies.

Dad answered on the first ring. "To what do I owe this delight?" he said, his mood even better than usual on this warm summer day.

I told him what Galen had just told me, and my dad guffawed before saying, "I knew it. I knew she couldn't resist."

"Clearly there is a story here," I said. "Spill."

Dad explained that given Thomas's somewhat ambiguous sexual orientation and gender identity – they went by "them" and sometimes dressed in women's clothes and sometimes in men's – Mrs. Riordan had been dropping hints that she thought Dad and Thomas were having an affair since they often had coffee and then stopped by the post office after their "dates."

"Her homophobia and gossip-mongering were so ugly that Thomas and I decided to put her in her place," Dad said, and I could hear the edge of anger in his voice.

"By giving her more to talk about?" I asked.

"By catching her in the act." He cleared his throat. "Now, thanks to you we can help people's privacy remain intact."

"Dad, she could go to jail!" I said, suddenly worried that my dad had opened a can of worms that he didn't really want squiggling around.

"Oh, we're not going to report her, Harvey." He cleared his throat. "But a solid conversation about privacy and about gossip with a hint of a threat of reporting it to her supervisors should do the trick." I could almost hear the glee in his voice. My dad wasn't much of a confrontational guy, but cross someone he loved – and he definitely loved his friend Thomas – and you would see his wrath.

"Let me know how it goes?" I said.

"Of course. I'll stop by later." He hung up, and I imagined he was already calling Thomas to plan their confrontation with Mrs. Riordan.

That had been almost a week ago, and while the rumors had slowed down a little bit, I still kept expecting to hear that Mrs. Riordan had been fired or something. Dad and Thomas had told her directly that she had no business reading anyone else's mail, that they knew she had been doing so given what people had said she told them – things she could only know if she'd read the letters directly – and that if they heard she was continuing to exhibit that behavior, they would have to report her.

"She didn't even bat an eye," Dad had said when he told me. "It was like we'd just said, 'If you keep catching butterflies and breaking their wings, you're going to be in big trouble.'"

"That woman," Mom had spat over her latte that afternoon in the café. "She's despicable." Mom was clearly much more upset about the rumors than dad, and I guess I might have been too if someone was saying things that questioned the solidity of my fifty-year marriage. "Maybe you should report her." Mom added.

Dad shook his head. "I'm not willing to do that unless I hear that she's been opening more mail. If I get word of that, though, Thomas and I won't hesitate." His jaw was set, and I knew he meant business. He didn't want to ruin a woman's career. "Thomas is livid. He thought calling her out would cause her to have some sort of remorse or at least guilt, but the fact that she seemed totally unfazed has him furious."

Now, though, a week after she had been called out, Mrs. Riordan was still gossiping away in the post office. She told my best friend and roommate Mart that Susie, the high school valedictorian, was going to have to put off college for a year while she dealt with an addiction problem, and our friend Kate had been subjected to a long story about Ms. Elmira's psoriasis and how it was the reason she had never married. The woman was shameless.

But we hadn't heard any more about her opening mail, so we had no recourse to speak to her. Gossiping wasn't a crime, but it sure was ugly. And now that I knew where the source – or at least one of them - of the information train in St. Marin's was, I made a commitment to mail anything personal from Easton when I ran errands. I didn't want my business to be spread around town.

Not that I had a lot of personal business that involved the

postal service, mind you. My dating life was completely dormant, which was actually fine. Mostly. And all of my best friends and family lived here in town, so my mail use was very limited, especially since I did most of my business for the bookstore via the internet. Still, I wasn't even going to use the mail to send my customer's special erotica orders if Mrs. Riordan might get wind of it.

It was Monday, and after another customer gave me a sympathetic squeeze of the forearm, I decided to stop thinking about Margie Riordan and focus on the new release book displays. My assistant manager, Marcus, had already begun to put the new titles on the front tables, and he did a stellar job. But given how much I had loved the publisher's advance copy of *Once There Were Wolves* by Charlotte McConaghy, I had decided to do a full window display featuring that book and several other wolf-related titles.

I had my fair share of werewolf books to choose from, but I decided to forego that trope and stick with wolf metaphors and books by women. Cate, a photographer who managed the local art co-op up the road, had crafted a large cut-out of a wolf and then used various photographs of wolves to create an image from images for the display. I put that piece of art at the edge of the window, as if the animal was stalking in. Then, I arranged stacks of McConaghy's book with copies of *Women Who Run With Wolves*, *A Wolf Called Wander*, and several other wolf-related titles, both fiction and nonfiction, into a forest-like display with streaming tendrils of crepe paper adding just the right touch of green.

Marcus joined me on the sidewalk outside as I was looking at my creation, and he whistled, "Darn, Harvey. This is beautiful and creepy. I like it."

I smiled. He was right. It was a little menacing, but honestly, I felt like women needed to be feared just a bit more in our society, so I was okay with that. *Let people know we are fierce*, I thought. "Thanks," I said. "Any more titles you want to add?" He studied the display, and I could see him flipping through the thousands of books he'd read in his mind's catalog. "I can't think of anything off-hand, but I'll let you know."

As he headed back inside, I studied the window once more and then started to follow him. Just then, I heard a scream from up the street and saw a young woman bolt out of the post office up the block. "Call 911! She's hurt!" she shouted toward me.

I didn't hesitate and took out my phone to dial the fastest help I knew. "Tuck," I said when the sheriff answered the phone. "Something's wrong at the post office."

"On my way," he said.

I sprinted up the road as soon as he hung up, and after talking with the woman who had screamed to see if I could comfort her, I stepped into the post office, careful to use my sleeve to open the door.

There, slumped against the counter, was Margie Riordan, and I didn't think she was simply hurt.

2

I jogged back outside and was glad to see that the young woman who had found Margie was still there. "The sheriff is on his way," I said as I led her to a brick flowerbed in front of the office so that we could both sit down. She was shaking. I knew, firsthand, that finding a body could be a very unnerving and terrifying experience.

As we sat there, I tried to look casual so that the townspeople and tourists walking by would think two friends were just sitting and talking, but my ruse was blown when my friend Symeon, Mart's boyfriend and chef at the local French restaurant, started to head into the post office after waving and smiling at me. "You can't go in, Sy," I said.

He stopped and turned back to me. "Are they closed?" He looked at his watch.

"No. Something has happened." I swung my eyes to the young woman who was still shivering beside me. "Tuck is on his way."

Symeon stared at the post office door for a minute and then came and joined us on the short wall. "Anything I can do?"

I gave my head a little shake. "No. Not now." I didn't want to tell him about how pale Margie had looked or that I thought I had seen blood on her chest. The woman who had found her was too upset to handle more information of that nature. Fortunately, Tuck and deputy Jared Watson arrived in two police cruisers after just a minute or two more. "Sorry it took us so long. We were over at the high school doing a routine walk-through," Watson said as he caught my eye and tilted his head toward the young woman.

"She found Margie, um, like that." I turned my head toward the post office door that Tuck was just now walking through. "She's pretty upset."

Watson returned to his car and came back with a Pepsi. "Here, drink this," he said as he sat down on the other side of the woman I was still comforting. "It will help with the shock."

I looked over at the deputy and smiled. He was a very kind man. Cute, too, and when he smiled back at me, I felt my heart kick.

Symeon shifted next to me and cleared his throat, reminding me to break the eye contact that Watson and I had held a moment too long. When I glanced over at him, he hid his smile.

Tuck stepped back out of the post office. "Watson, we need to make that call."

The deputy stood, walked over to the driver's side door of his cruiser, and leaned in to get the radio. His voice was quiet, but I thought I heard the word "dead" as he spoke. He was calling the coroner.

When Watson came back over, he knelt in front of the young woman and said, "I need to ask you a few questions, but first, is there someone I can call to come get you?"

She looked up at him and said, "My girlfriend." She handed over her phone, and I saw Watson scroll through the contacts until he found the right one. Then he pressed the name and stepped away to ask her to come join her girlfriend at the post office.

"What's your name?" I asked the woman beside me, who looked a bit better after the soda. Her light-brown skin was getting some pink back in it, and she wasn't shaking as hard. "Lane," she said. "Thank you. I'm sorry—"

"Stop, no need to apologize," I said. "You had a shock. I'm glad I was here."

"Me, too," she said as she took another sip from the can.

As Watson walked back over, I said to Lane, "Deputy Watson—"

He interrupted me and met my eye again, "Jared. Call me Jared."

I smiled and nodded and said, "Jared here is a good guy. He just needs to know what you saw. Are you up to talking to him?"

Lane nodded and then stood to walk with Jared a few feet away.

Symeon bumped my shoulder and said, "Jared, huh?"

I sighed. "Apparently," I said trying to act nonchalant and knowing full well that Sy was going to call Mart as soon as he walked away. Now, my evening would be consumed by my best friend's ceaseless scheming to get me a date with the deputy. Mart was amazing, always supportive, but she knew I wanted a partner, someone who really got me, and since she had found that in Sy, she was even more relentless in Operation Harvey Hook-up, as she called it.

"I like him," Symeon said matter-of-factly as he stood.

Tuck came out of the post office again. "Anyone else been in there?" he asked Symeon and me.

"Not through this door," I said. "I stopped Symeon on his way in, and no one else has come up."

Tuck nodded. "You okay?" he asked me.

"Yeah, always a shock, you know, but yeah, I'm okay." Now that I wasn't taking care of Lane, the adrenaline was wearing off. I held up my hands and saw they were beginning to shake. "I better sit back down though."

"I'll call Mart," Symeon said.

I smiled. "Okay, that might be good. You have to get back to Chez Cuisine don't you?"

Sy looked at his watch again. "Yeah. Shift starts, well, now, but Max will understand why I'm a few minutes late. I'll wait with you until Mart gets here."

"Thanks," I said. "Let me just call Marcus and Rocky so they know why I'm not back at the store." I pulled out my phone, and when it went to voicemail, probably because Marcus was with a customer, I hung up and dialed the café. Rocky, the café manager, answered on the second ring. "Mug Shots," she said.

She'd recently chosen that name for the café, and I loved it. Now that she was the full owner of the place – we'd executed a contract for sale with me getting rent instead of a cut of sales every month – she was doing everything to make it her own. The name was just the first step.

"Hey Rocky. There's been an incident at the post office. I may be a while," I said and then quickly told her about Margie. "You guys okay?"

"Absolutely," she said. "Are you?"

"Yeah. Symeon is here, and Mart is on her way. I'll see you in a bit," I said before I hung up.

While Jared took Lane's statement and Tuck, presumably, reviewed more of the crime scene, Sy and I sat quietly on the brick wall. I remembered sitting like this when I was little and waiting for the school bus with a girl named Nora who lived down the street. We'd never been friends, but there was a kind of camaraderie of waiting, and it was nice to share that with Symeon now.

Within minutes, Mart pulled up, wet brown hair tugged back in a pony tail and a worried expression on her face. She kissed Sy on the cheek at the same moment she pulled me into a tight hug. "Not again, Harvey."

I sighed. I had found dead bodies a few times now, and my friends were beginning to joke that I had some kind of psychic connection to those who had just crossed over. Our friend Stephen had even taken to calling me "Love," as in Jennifer Love Hewitt, the star of Ghost Whisperer.

But I didn't think I was psychic. I just thought I paid attention and happened to work downtown, where it seemed the murderers of St. Marin's liked to find their victims. That was a morbid thought for sure.

Symeon headed off to work, and Mart took his seat on the low wall beside me. "You okay?" she asked as she put her arm around me and let me set my head on her shoulder.

"I am." I lifted my head and turned toward her. "You know I don't want this, right? I'm not trying to find all these bodies."

She whipped around to face me. "Of course you aren't, Harvey." Her face moved from annoyed to sad in a split second. "I'm sorry for what I said before. I didn't mean to imply it was your fault. It's not. I just wish you didn't have to be the one to find every corpse in St. Marin's." She winked at me. "But these people are lucky when you do. You care, Harvey. That's why we all worry about you."

I sighed. "I know." I let the silence settle around us for a bit before I said, "Poor Margie."

Mart cleared her throat. "Yes, I suppose, but also that woman was awful. I don't mean to speak ill of the dead . . ." She didn't finish her sentence.

"Yeah, she definitely got her nose in where it didn't belong," I added as I felt the last of the adrenaline leave my hands and feet. I was suddenly so sleepy.

"In what way?" Tuck said as she walked up behind us. "What do you mean, Harvey?"

I groaned. "Sorry, Tuck. I didn't mean to imply anything specific, just that she was in a perfect position to be the town gossip since she saw everyone's mail."

Tuck nodded. "Okay, but you know I know the rumors, too, right? About her opening mail? We've been asked to investigate several times, but we never found any evidence."

Watson walked back over after taking Lane's statement and helping her into her girlfriend's car. He added, "She was sort of like the mafia. We were going to have to catch her on the postal version of tax evasion, I think."

"Looks like somebody took care of that problem for you," Mart said quietly.

"I wish I'd known you were investigating. She actually confessed to opening my dad's mail a few weeks ago," I said.

Mart pinched my arm hard and shot me a look from the corner of her eye. "But that was all a joke, right?" Her voice was strained, as if she was trying to push the words toward the center of my brain.

I instantly realized my mistake and tried to laugh like it was, actually, all a joke, but I could tell from the look on Tuck's and Jared's faces that they weren't buying it.

"Tell us what happened, Harvey," Tuck said as he took his notebook out of his shirt pocket. "In detail."

This time my groan was much louder, but I explained what had happened with Dad's and Thomas's letters, about how she had confessed to Galen. "I'm sure they'd all be happy to talk to you."

"Good. I'll call them now. Do they still have the letters?" Jared asked.

I shrugged. "I have no idea." I didn't like the idea that my dad or my friends were about to be questioned in relation to a murder, but I also knew that it was better to tell the truth and get it all out front than it was to have Tuck or Jared find out about the prank on Margie later. "Galen is probably at home; he does most of his social media set-up on Mondays, and I know Dad will be."

My dad had a routine that was almost as regimented as the one he'd had when he was working. Monday was his "round the house" day, as he called it. He took out the garbage, did a thorough cleaning of the kitchen and bathrooms (his part of the labor division my parents put in place as soon as they bought their condo), and paid bills. This evening, he and Mom would go out to a nice dinner as a reward for their responsible choices to begin the week. The routine never varied. Until today.

I stood and said, "Do you need more from me right now? If not, I should probably get back to the shop." I waved my hand up the street and glanced longingly toward the respite of my store.

"I think we have what we need from you, Harvey," Tuck said, "but don't leave town." He winked as he spoke knowing that, first, I would recognize the standard cop line from every police procedural I watched and, second, that I couldn't leave town and keep my business going.

"If you're okay, I should get over to the winery. We're releasing a new reserve today, and the press are swarming," Mart said as she gave me a hug.

I nodded. "Someday, you will explain to me what a swarm looks like at a wine party. Are the photographers wearing cravats? Are there cocktail dresses?" I smirked at my best friend.

"Hardy, har, har," Mart said as she headed toward her car. She blew me a kiss as she climbed in and drove away.

Tuck had already driven away, and so Jared and I stood there, awkwardly, looking at our shoes. "I guess I'll head back," I finally said.

"Want company for the walk?" he asked with a blush.

Given that I could almost see the individual petals on the marigolds blooming in the planter boxes outside my store, it wasn't much of a walk really, but still, I smiled. "Sure. I always enjoy good company."

The blush on his cheeks darkened further as he turned and matched my pace up the sidewalk. I was walking a bit more slowly than usual, I realized, but I didn't pick up speed. This guy was cute and kind, and he was probably going to interrogate my father soon. So I figured that it was a win-win if I flirted a little.

"So you come here often?" I said and felt myself wither a little. My flirting skills were definitely subpar.

He laughed. "Almost every day, actually. I live just around the corner." He pointed toward the river side of town into a neighborhood of cute Victorian houses. "I bought one of the fixer uppers back there."

I grinned. "That's a fun project, I bet. Keep you busy?"

"Only if having to refinish all the original pumpkin pine floors and hunt down an antique mantel counts as busy. I think of it as fun," he said with a smile.

"Actually, that does sound fun, except no one wants me to manage a floor sander unless they're thinking of installing a firefighter's pole through the floor. If so, I'm your girl to cut the hole." I took a deep breath. Apparently, my flirting game had a good rebound.

"How are you with a hammer?" he asked.

"Depends on who you ask. I think I'm amazing. Most actual hammer users think I could use some work. Want to give me lessons?" I blushed at my brashness. We had just gone right from casual to full-on flirting, and from the grin on his face, he seemed in for it.

"Definitely," he said, "but only if I can cook you dinner first."

My head felt light, but thankfully we were at the door of my store. Otherwise, I might have just swooned right there. "That sounds great. I think at this point I'm supposed to take your phone and put in my digits or something."

He cackled. "At our age, the word *digits* calls up lost fingers or toes, but maybe I could call you here at the store later to get your number and set up a time for our, um, date. Is it okay that I call it a date?"

"I'd be disappointed if you didn't," I said with what I hoped was a saucy wink as I stepped into my store.

I made my way directly to the café because I required caffeine to recover my wits and, ironically, slow my heart rate. "Vanilla latte. STAT," I said.

"So the hot officer and you looked like you were having a good chat?" Rocky said as she steamed my milk and tried to look nonchalant.

I leaned forward on the counter. "We have a date," I whispered.

She smiled. "That's awesome, Harvey. When?"

"He's calling later to set up a time to make me dinner." A wave of anxiety washed over me. "What do you wear to someone's house for dinner and hammering lessons?"

Rocky looked up. "Is that some kind of euphemism?" she said with a taste of concern in her words.

I blushed for the third time. "No, he's restoring his house, and I said I was pretty good with a hammer." When Rocky smirked, I rolled my eyes. "Stop. I'm hoping to help him do some home repair," I finished.

"I bet you are," Rocky said as she slid my drink across the counter. "I. Bet. You. Are."

I shook my head and walked back to the store, where the customers were busy threading in and around the shelves. An older woman with the most amazing crown of braids and super cute cat-eye glasses stopped me and said, "Do you have an African American literature section?"

I shook my head. "I don't. I decided I didn't want to segregate my books that way, BUT I do have a lot of books by African American authors shelved in the store. Are you looking for something in particular?"

The woman smiled. "Actually, yes, do you have African American romance novels?" She grinned.

"Totally. Come this way? Anyone in particular?"

"Yes, I want to read that book from Reese's book club. The one about July is it?"

I smiled. "*Seven Days In June.* So good. It's right here," I pointed to where we had three copies faced out. "You'll love it." As I turned to go, I saw her scanning the shelves. This woman was a romance lover, I could tell. She'd be to the counter soon with a few books.

Sure enough, my newest customer bought six romance novels, and while I wasn't a big romance reader, I still commended her choices. I wasn't ever going to be down on anyone who read a lot, no matter what they read. I didn't fault non-readers either, but I definitely related to people who disappeared into stories most deeply.

That was one of the reasons I had opened my store – I just wanted to be around all these bibliophiles. I loved watching people read books. I loved talking about books. I loved buying books. I was living my dream in all the senses, especially since our financial returns had been really solid for more than a year now.

I couldn't think of one thing I wanted to change about the store except maybe that I wanted more room. *Someday,* I thought. *Someday.*

Today, though, I decided to keep my mind focused on the here and now and do what I did best – sell books. As I wandered through the history section, I caught Marcus's eye as he talked to an older, gray-haired man with a deep tan and a beautiful cane. They were discussing books about food, and I heard enough of the customer's side of the conversation to know that he was a making a change to a more plant-based diet. I wasn't surprised when Marcus recommended Michael Pollan's *The Omnivore's Dilemma* and *Eating Animals* by Jonathan Safran Foer. I knew they were two books that had influenced him to become vegan, and they were good ones, too. I wasn't going vegan anytime soon, but reading them, at Marcus's suggestion, had definitely gotten me to cut back on my meat consumption and choose my sources of meat wisely.

Most of the reading chairs were full around the store, and I gave people gentle passing smiles as I wandered by, eager to have them know I was happy for them to read as long as they wished. In the children's section, a little boy and his mom were scooping up all the books in the Mysterious Benedict Society series, and I couldn't help but praise their choice. I loved those books.

His mom smiled at me and said, "I really want to watch the show, but Xavier insists we read the books first."

"Good man," I said. "I always read the book first."

He grinned a gap-toothed smile and followed me to the register, where he removed three crisp twenty dollar bills from his Harry Potter wallet and handed them to me. He was buying all four books in the series plus the prequel and the puzzle book, so I used my owner's prerogative and sold them all for the cost of the four main books. Any fan that loyal deserved a discount.

His mother thanked me, and Xavier made his way, without a misstep, to the front door while reading the first volume. I loved that boy immediately.

The rest of the afternoon went along similarly with Marcus and I roaming, straightening, and recommending while Rocky frothed away in the café. By the time Marcus left and Rocky's new cashier, Cecilia, came in at four, I had almost forgotten that I found a body.

My blissful lapse in memory came to an end shortly before five when my mother stomped into the store, stood in front of me at the register, and said, "How could you, Harvey?"

3

I stared at my mother, mouth open, for a few seconds as I tried to figure out what exactly I had done. There had been a time when "breathing" might have been the right answer, at least in my mind, but over the past year or more, we had gotten closer and closer as she loosened up her expectations for her daughter and as my business got more and more successful. By some twist of universal goodness, my goals and hers were aligning, which helped heal a few decades of distance between us.

Now, though, the look on her face was the exact same one she had worn countless times when I had told her things about my life that disappointed her – that I was going to be a nonprofit fundraiser, that I was moving to San Francisco, that I had left my negligent husband, that I was opening a bookstore – I could go on. My defenses went up immediately, and I folded my arms in front of my chest. "What are you talking about?"

"You told Tuck that your father might have killed Margie Riordan. What do you mean, 'What am I talking about?' That should be obvious." Her voice was getting louder and louder, and my first instinct was to take her into the back room to continue the conversation. But even though Cecilia was a great new addition to the store, she wasn't yet trained to run the register over in the bookstore side of things. So I had to stay put.

"Mom, first, lower your voice. Secondly, I said no such thing."

She harrumphed and shook her head. "Then why did Tuck say that you told him about that silly stunt your father and Thomas played on Margie?"

"Because I did," I said matter-of-factly.

Before I could explain further, Mom's eyes grew wide, and she threw her hands in the air. "How dare you treat your father this way." She was practically shouting now, and not a few of the customers were looking our direction.

Fortunately, at that moment, my friend Elle stepped into the store with the flower delivery for the week. She'd wanted to wait an extra day until her zinnias were fully open before she made her weekly delivery, and I couldn't have been more grateful for a delay than I was at that moment.

She took one look at me and my mother and stepped behind the register. "I've got this," she said.

I nodded, grabbed my mother by the elbow, and dragged her to the back room. She resisted, but as she passed the staring customers, she grew more and more compliant. My mother didn't like to make a scene, unless it was for a good cause. If she was raising money as a volunteer for one of the many charities she supported, she'd cause all the ruckus she could, but family business was a different matter.

Now, seated with a cup of water at our staff break table, she was beginning to regain control of herself. As she took a series of deep breaths, I said, "Mom, I was there when a woman found Margie's body. In the course of talking to Tuck and," I paused to choose my words, careful to not bring something else into this conversation, "and Deputy Watson, they mentioned that they had tried to find evidence of the postmistress reading people's mail."

Mom's face relaxed. "And you mentioned how she had told your friend Galen about steaming open your father and Thomas's letters." She sighed.

"Right, and then because I didn't want any suspicion to be cast on Dad or Thomas by my silence, I told them the whole story. My intention was to keep Dad away from suspicion, not shine more on him." I huffed and sat down. Even though what I said was true, I knew that what had actually happened mattered – apparently, my father becoming a murder suspect – far more than what I had wanted to happen, however. "So what happened?"

Mom sat back and sighed again. "Tuck came by the house and asked your dad about Margie Riordan. He didn't tell your father that she was murdered," she paused, "and I guess I see why, but it felt like a trap." She pulled her gray hair tight into a bunch at the back of her head and let it go.

"Dad told him the truth, right?"

Mom's eyes snapped to mine. "Of course. You know your father always tells the truth, sometimes too baldly. Besides he had nothing to hide."

I nodded. "I know he didn't. That's why I wasn't worried."

"Well, after Tuck finally told him that Margie was murdered, your father was told he is a person of interest and so is Thomas." Mom glared at me before she looked down. "But I guess I can't blame you for that."

I took my mom's hands. She was a mess, and I couldn't fault her. I was feeling a bit of a wreck again myself. "You know that Tuck will find the real killer, Mom."

She swallowed. "I do know, but the idea that anyone could think your father capable . . ." She grew quiet, and for the first time in my life, I saw tears in her eyes.

I grabbed her in a big hug. "Tuck doesn't think he is a

murderer, Mom. He just has to do his job." A thought flashed through my mind, and for a split second, I thought about sharing it with Mom but decided better of it. "He will find out who did this, and Dad's name will be completely cleared."

Mom's chest shuddered against me. "I know. And he wasn't arrested or anything, so I guess no one else knows."

I pulled back and looked my mother in the fact. "Right. And we will keep it that way."

"Okay," she said, "but you'll help find out the truth, won't you?"

I suppressed my own shudder and nodded. "Of course. Do you want me to keep this completely to myself, or would you like me to ask for help?

Mom studied her hands. "Your friends know your father, and they like him, right?"

"Of course," I said. "I'm pretty sure Walter or Cate would marry him if they were single." My friends definitely had a man-crush on my dad, and when it wasn't creepy, it was kind of cute.

"Then let's ask them to help." She met my eyes again, and this time, her gaze was soft and scared. "The sooner the better."

I took my phone out of my pocket and looked at the time. "We close in 90 minutes. Let's all meet here at seven. Are you up for getting us a main course and some drinks?" My mother coped with hardship best by being active.

"Absolutely," she said and stood up. "I'll run up to the Greek diner and get us a feast." She was halfway to the door when she stopped and turned around. "I'm sorry, Harvey."

I walked to her and said, "Forget about it. Just get me an extra piece of spanakopita, okay?"

She smiled and went out the door as I looked back at my phone, found our group text, and told everyone we had an emergency dinner at the store at seven. The responses were fast and quick, especially since I said Mom was bringing all the food, and aside from Henri, who was on call to staff the art co-op, and Woody, who wanted an update but said he had to be somewhere else that night, everyone said they'd be here. We'd have this situation cleared up in no time.

WHEN I MADE my way back to the desk a few moments later, Elle had not only staffed the register but also tidied the shelves beneath it and made a gorgeous arrangement of zinnias and bachelor's buttons for the front table. "Thank you, Elle," I said. "Really."

"No problem. It's fun to clean at someone else's place, and it gave me time to recommend a couple of great gardening books, too." She tilted her chin at a gorgeous Asian woman in a linen skirt who was browsing our gardening section. "She wants to start a dahlia garden."

I laughed. "Well then, how fortuitous that she came in while the cut flower expert was on duty." Elle grew the most amazing flowers and sold them to store owners, florists, and bridal parties at a pace she could barely keep up. Fortunately, her business was so good that she'd hired on some new staff for the actual farming and was beginning a new arm of her business as a bulb provider via a CSA-type structure. People would sign-up for her bulb boxes for the fall and spring, and she'd provide a variety of flowers for them to plant in their own yards. She was calling her new business, "Spread the Bloom," and from what I'd heard, it was going very well.

"Since I might as well just stay here until we eat later," she said, "want to give me a sneak peek of what we're going to be talking about."

I took a deep breath and told her about Margie Riordan, Dad and Thomas, and Mom's concern about Dad's reputation.

When I finished whispering the news to her, she looked at

me and said, "Your mom is so sweet, but really, your dad could not kill someone. He might get his shirt dirty."

I guffawed so loudly that several customers spun around to stare, and I had to apologize. "You're right," I said turning back to Elle. "He's a little like Elijah from *The Originals*. Always with the handkerchief and the washing of his hands."

"I have no idea who Elijah is, but yes. Also, is that one of you and Mart's vampire shows?" Elle said with a roll of her eyes.

I smiled. "You know it." Mart and I had been on a bit of a binge for the past few weeks. First, we had finished *The Vampire Diaries* and fought valiantly for our respective brothers. I was firmly on Team Stefan, which was fine with Mart since she had a deep affection for Damon. Then, we had jumped ahead in the universe timeline and watched *Legacies*, and now, we were four seasons deep in *The Originals* and agreed it was the best series so far, although we were probably going to go to blows over Langdon Kirby when the new season of *Legacies* came out.

Elle, however, preferred her TV of the actual reality kind. Documentaries, PBS gardening shows, and the occasional British murder mystery. Of course, *Rosemary and Thyme* was her favorite British mystery show, and I couldn't say I blamed her. Those women were delightful.

Between customers and flower arrangements for the café, Elle and I snarked at each other about our TV viewing habits – I said she was prudish and a snob, and she retorted by saying I was low-brow. Neither of us was really wrong, and it was all in good fun. So by the time we closed up shop, and I walked Cecilia to her car in the lot behind the row of stores – something I insisted on doing every night because of the rash of murders we'd had in town – I was feeling pretty downright jovial.

When Mom knocked on the front door with her arms full of the most amazing smelling food, I felt my mood tick up another notch. That is, until I saw my dad's face. He looked drawn and pale behind the tower of recyclable trays stacked in his arms. I took his load, set it on the register counter, and I immediately hugged him. My dad wasn't much of a hugger, but he grabbed me tight and didn't let go for a few moments.

When I pulled back, I looked up at him and held his gaze. He wasn't ready to talk about things, I could tell, but I wanted him to see how much I believed in him, how much I knew he was innocent. I hoped his wan smile meant he did.

Our friends were soon streaming in the door, Stephen and Walter with a mini-bar full of delights for our relaxing pleasure, Cate and Lucas with some of his signature cupcakes, and Pickle and Bear with an assortment of pickled vegetables courtesy of Pickle's new hobby that he'd taken up as an homage to his nickname. Apparently, our friends could not follow directions about food, but I couldn't say I was complaining. Between the Greek salads, the falafel, the gyros, the spanakopita, and all this other deliciousness, I thought I might just sleep at the store tonight so I could eat until I couldn't walk.

The mood was light as we all filled our plates and took our usual spots on the chairs and rug in the fiction section. I would never have dreamed up this group of friends or our regular picnic dinners in my store would have been a thing when I opened my business, but I was sure glad it was now.

Still, as soon as we settled in to eat, the mood dipped a bit. Thomas had come in a few minutes earlier, and while he had been cordial when I said hello, he was definitely not his usual, chipper self. And for some reason, Mart and Symeon were a bit subdued as well.

As we ate, I waited a bit to see if Mom or Dad wanted to explain why we were all here, but when they both refused to look up from their plates when I tried to catch their eyes, I decided I needed to take the lead. So I did.

I began by telling everyone about Margie Riordan's murder,

told them about Thomas and Dad's prank on the postmistress, and then explained that Dad and Thomas were now "persons of interest" in the case. The story of the cologne-scented letters had garnered a few smiles from our friends, but as soon as I said the men were suspects, all chiding stopped and the mood grew darker still.

"Symeon's a suspect, too," Mart said as she met my eye. "He spent the afternoon at the police station."

"What?! Why?" I said. "You were coming into the post office *after* Margie was dead. That makes no sense."

Symeon shook his head. "It does when you know I threatened her yesterday." His voice was stark, and the silence filling the room even more bleak.

I looked from him to Mart and back to him. "Why did you threaten her?"

Symeon looked down at the nearly-full plate in his lap. "I can't say."

My eyes shot to Mart, and she shrugged and shook her head. "He won't tell me either," she said.

"I didn't kill her," Symeon said quietly.

"Of course not," Mart added as she rubbed his arm. "But why won't you explain so we can clear your name?"

"I have my reasons," he said and then stood, dropped his paper plate in the trashcan by the door, and let himself out.

Mart started to follow him, but Stephen pushed her back into her seat. "Let me go. Maybe he'll talk to someone he doesn't know as well."

I didn't think that made much sense, but Mart nodded and sat back down as she watched Stephen follow Symeon out the door.

Cate leaned forward toward Mart. "You have no idea what that's about?"

"None. I can't think of a single reason Symeon would threaten Margie. He's such a tender guy." Mart sounded like she was going to cry, and I stood up and went to sit beside her in Symeon's chair.

"He is, Mart," I said, "and he didn't do this." I sure hoped my voice sounded more sure than I felt.

EVENTUALLY, Stephen slipped back into a chair, but when he didn't say anything, I decided to trust my friends, both Mart and him, to handle the situation as they felt best and didn't ask any more questions.

But we did try to determine who else might have a motive to kill the postmistress. There was the high school history teacher who got tried for assault when Margie revealed that he had been the one sending threatening letters to the principal. But that guy was in jail, and he didn't seem like the type to have "connections" so he went low on our list.

Then, Pickle mentioned that one his clients had her own reasons for wishing ill on Margie. Of course, he didn't tell us a name or any particulars, but assured us he would look into it.

The most promising suspect, however, was a real estate broker in town, Edgar Levine, whose prospect of building a luxury casino at the edge of St. Marin's had been foiled when Margie leaked the word of his purchases to, well, everyone in town. Levine had been hoping to scoop up the unprotected wetlands north of town for a steal, but once the news spread, the value of those lots suddenly doubled and the local environmental groups had gotten involved. The sales were soon halted as research studies began.

The broker had made no secret of his anger. I could still remember Levine screaming at his assistant through the phone one day while he got a coffee in Mug Shots. "You are an incompetent bozo," Levine had said. "Didn't you think to use unmarked envelopes when we wrote to the town clerk's office about who owned those parcels?"

I remembered the conversation vividly because I'd had to go over and ask him to either lower his voice or leave. He had left, but only after slinging his coffee across the counter to Rocky and nearly burning her wrist in the process. Now, as I thought about what Levine might have done, about the way it was hurting my parents and Symeon, my anger was rising. I channeled my fury into an aggressive stomp back to the breakroom and a forceful pushing of my whiteboard into the front of the store. I had used this board once to try and solve a murder, and I figured it was time to use it again.

I began writing up all the suspects – Dad, Thomas, Symeon, Pickle's client, Levine – but I immediately crossed through Dad, Thomas, and Symeon. They were not murderers, and anyone who thought that was a fool. I took a step back as I realized that meant that Tuck was a fool, and I knew that wasn't true. I stared at the board as the cognitive dissonance in my brain paralyzed me.

Lucas stood and took the markers from me and rewrote the names, the motive for each suspect, including a big question mark for Symeon, as well as any knowledge of opportunity that we had. By the time he was done, I realized we knew a whole bunch of nothing, and I felt a jolt of sympathy for Tuck, who probably didn't know much more than we did at this point.

Unfortunately, my judgment hadn't been great, and I had set up the board facing the front window. Fortunately, if belatedly, Marcus had a clearer mind and gently turned me and the board around so that only a black space could be seen from the street.

As I stared past the board to the front window, I saw the election sign we had hung months ago to show our support for our friend's bid for sheriff. Tuck knew we were gathering, but he'd declined stating a conflict of interest. We knew it would put him in awkward position to be with Dad, Thomas, and

Symeon. Still, I trusted Tuck, and I knew he would do right by everyone, including Margie.

I took a deep breath, took out my phone, and took a picture of the board. "I'm sending this to Tuck, if you're all okay with that." Dad and Thomas nodded, and then Mart gave me a quick thumbs up. I sent the image with a note that said, "Doing our thing. Hope it helps."

Tuck's reply was almost instant. "It does. But don't get too involved, Harvey. I have got this, okay? Trust me?"

Tears pricked my eyes and I typed, "I do. But hurry, okay?"

"Absolutely," was his reply.

With the murder board filled out as best we could, there wasn't much left for us to talk about, so my friends began clean up, and Rocky made a fresh pot of decaf for everyone so that they could have an iced coffee for the ride home.

I pushed the murder board back to the storeroom and stood staring at it until my mom came in. I shook myself out of my melancholy and put my arm around her shoulders. It seemed like maybe she was getting shorter. "We're going to figure this out, Mom."

She squeezed my waist. "I have no doubt."

4

M om and Dad left after almost everyone else, but they finally made their way out, even though I could tell the idea of going home didn't really appeal. In what I hoped would be a help, I suggested they check out the new TV show *Clarkson's Farm* so that they could laugh, like I had, at how a car enthusiast approached farming with a Lamborghini tractor. It would be good distraction if they could manage to let themselves be distracted.

Marcus and Rocky lingered as I did the final closing duties, each of them busying themselves enough to assuage any of the guilt I might have had about their presence. By the time Marcus set the alarm and I locked the door behind the three of us, the store was spic and span. The thought of coming into the shop with a completely clean slate of work really soothed something in my spirit that was far too anxious as it was.

Fortunately, Mayhem and Taco had eaten their fair share of gyro meat from dinner, and so they weren't too eager to get home. So when I assured my two colleagues that I would text them when I arrived there safely, the two dogs and I started our leisurely walk.

As we crossed the first street beyond the shop, I followed a whim and turned right. It felt like it might be nice to just see Jared's house, even if I had not yet answered the message he left with Marcus at the store a few hours earlier. I had hoped to call him before we closed up to make plans, but the day had gotten away from me. Plus, if I was honest, I just didn't know if I could start a new romance with all this hanging over my head.

My thoughts flew ahead, as they always did when a new venture loomed, and I let myself be distracted by questions about where Jared and I would live if we got married, about whether he had a dog and whether or not that dog would get along with my dogs, about his potential fear of dogs. I was so caught up in my anxiety about the future of the man I had yet to spend even one hour with that it took me a minute to realize that someone was calling my name as I walked.

When finally I shook myself out of my fog and pinpointed the voice in the dusk, I found myself staring up at Jared himself. He was sitting at the edge of a beautiful, deep porch that came off a gorgeous purple Victorian house. "Whew, glad you answered. I was afraid your body had been abducted by aliens, and I was going to have to jump off this porch and force them to give you back."

I grinned. "If anything is going to take over my body, it's the spirit of a long-dead witch who was created from the union of two tribes over 1,000 years ago."

"I'm pretty sure Klaus and Elijah defeated Inadu, so I think you're safe from that one." He laughed.

My smile grew even wider. "So Jackson or Elijah?" I asked, hoping this handsome, handy guy knew his vampire TV as well as he seemed.

"I'm a total Jackson in real life, but for TV romance, Elijah all the way. You?"

"You have to ask?" I pointed at his flannel shirt as he climbed down a ladder and walked over to the edge of the sidewalk into the front of his house. "I have a thing for woodsy types."

"Did I tell you my middle name is Jackson?" he said with a smirk.

"Is it now?" I said.

He ran a hand over his blonde hair and then along the five o'clock shadow that barely showed on his chin. "Not really, but I could grow this out." He looked up into the sky. "At least I think I could. Not sure what police regulations are about beards."

I laughed. "I like you beard or no beard," I said and found that I really meant it.

He blushed and ducked his head before finally looking up again and saying, "So what brings you this way?"

"I needed a little fresh air," I said, "and a certain police officer said he had a house over here. I was hoping I'd be able to tell which one by the type of flowers he grows." I glanced over at the soft beds of ferns and hostas he had tucked under the maples out front. "I would have thought you more a 'lawn only' kind of guy, actually, so it's a good thing you are outside."

He looked over at the beds. "That's all my mom. She's the plant expert. But I do pretty well at keeping things alive," he said. Then his face grew serious. "It was kind of a day, huh?"

I sighed as I adjusted the dogs' leashes in my hands. "You could say that."

"Sorry about your dad. I wish . . ."

I raised a hand to stop him. "Please. We all know you're doing your jobs. All I ask is that you act quickly."

He nodded. "From what I hear, you and your friends have helped us move along in the investigation." He held up his phone. "I saw your murder board."

I looked away in embarrassment. "Yeah, it's a thing I do sometimes. I need to process hard things out loud. Actually, I need to process all things out loud. And my friends indulge me." I studied his face. "But I'm surprised it was helpful."

"Yeah, I think it's okay that I tell you Tuck didn't know that one of Pickle's clients might be involved. Just got word that we're talking to her tomorrow."

"Oh?" It took every bit of self-control I had to not say, "Who is it?" But I held back and changed the subject. I wouldn't be able to resist asking questions if we stayed in this territory long. "Sorry I didn't return your call."

"Do *not* worry about that. I know how to find you." He winked at me, and I felt a thump in my chest.

"Well, we could set up dinner plans now if you want, save me some minutes on my phone." I smiled.

For a split second, Jared looked really confused, but then he caught my smirk and laughed. "1997 called and they want their calling card back," he said with a laugh. "What nights don't you close? Any night will work, but I go to bed kind of early, and I'd like as much of an evening with you as I can get."

I took a deep breath and said, "I'm done early tomorrow . . . if that's not too soon."

Jared grinned. "It's not too soon at all. Now, what don't you eat?"

"Seafood," I said and shrugged. "Go figure. I live in a water-side town, and I don't like the stuff."

"So stuffed crab and scallops it is," he joked. "How does a homemade lasagna with a fresh salad, garlic bread, and cannoli sound?"

Even though I was so full from dinner that I could have gone three days without eating, I almost groaned in delight at the idea of that meal. "That sounds just about perfect. Can I bring wine?"

"I like how you think," Jared said. "See you tomorrow. Five-thirty?"

I nodded and wrapped the dogs' leashes around my hand. "Looking forward to it."

"Me, too," he said as he leaned over and kissed my cheek." Be safe going home."

I smiled and led the dogs up the cross street by his house and toward home. Life was always so mixed up – so much hard and so much good at the same time. Tonight, though, I was going to focus on the good and imagine whether Jared would be wearing flannel and another day's growth of beard at dinner tomorrow.

WHEN I GOT HOME a few minutes later, Mart was already on the couch with a cozy throw on her lap and a new episode of *Glow Up* playing on the TV. The mug of hot tea – instead of her usual wine – in her hand told me that she was seeking comfort not escape tonight.

I changed into my pjs and climbed in next to her after shifting my cat Aslan out of the way. I spread the blanket over my legs as the dogs settled into the beds nearby. Unlike me, my best friend did not like to talk about everything right away, so I let myself get swept up in the make-up show and trusted she'd talk when she was ready.

Once the episode was over, she switched over to *The Originals*, and hit pause. "Symeon is all kind of messed up," she said. "But he won't talk to me."

I sighed. "That's weird, right? I mean he's pretty open usually, isn't he?"

"Completely. Whatever made him so angry at Margie, well, he just isn't explaining." She sighed. "He didn't kill her. I know that. I just wish he would tell me, or at least tell Tuck, what he was upset with her over."

I nodded. "Did you talk to Stephen?"

Mart's jaw tightened. "I did, and he knows but won't tell me either."

My anger surged. "What?! Why not?"

"He says that Symeon told him what was going on so that Stephen could assure us all that he hadn't done anything wrong. But that he also swore secrecy to Symeon." Mart's voice was laced with a combination of anger and sorrow. "I hate secrets," she whispered.

"I do, too. Want me to talk to Stephen?" I thought I could probably convince one of my oldest friends to give me the scoop if I explained how miserable Mart was.

"No," Mart said briskly before softening and saying, "Thank you, though. I don't want to put you, Stephen, or Symeon in that position. I'm just going to have to trust him."

I sighed. "Okay. But if you change your mind, I have ways of making people talk," I said in my best yet still terrible Russian accent. "Should we admire some gorgeous vampires?"

"Let's," she said and pressed play but then almost immediately pressed pause again. "Wait. Jared. What happened with Jared? Did you call him back?"

I'd texted Mart to tell her he had called as soon as I got his message, and I'd wanted to tell her about our conversation at his house as soon as I got home. But she clearly needed my support more than she needed my giddy, school-girlish news. Now that she's asked though, I found myself having to resist bouncing up and down on the couch.

"I ran into him on the way home," I said without meeting her eyes.

"Oh?" she said. "He was downtown? Maybe he was looking for you." She smirked.

"Well, not exactly," I said, still not meeting her gaze.

"What does that mean?" she said as she leaned closer.

"I saw him at his house," I whispered.

"You what?" she said. "You went to his house?"

I sighed. "Not exactly. I just wanted to see if I could figure out which one was his, and he was outside."

"So he caught you," she said with a laugh. "You're so smooth, Harvey."

"Like silk," I said in my best Barry-White voice, "silk that has been put through a paper shredder that is." I laughed. "Anyway, he's making me dinner at his house, which is gorgeous by the way, tomorrow night."

"Ooh, la la. The man cooks. Say no more." She smiled and picked up the remote before pausing the show again. "He does know you don't eat seafood, right?" Mart had been around at enough dinner parties and seafood restaurants where I'd subsisted on bread for the evening to know this was a big deal for me.

"He's making lasagna, salad, and garlic bread. Oh, and cannoli," I said, my mouth starting to water at just the thought.

"Seriously, woman? That is like your favorite meal." She turned back to the TV. "I expect you home by ten."

"Yes, Mother," I said and let myself disappear into Klaus's winsome smile.

THE NEXT MORNING, I was at the store super early because I was a buzzing with both excitement and worry. I was really looking forward to my date with Jared, but I was still concerned about my dad. Unfortunately, there wasn't much for me to do at the shop because of our tidying frenzy last night, so I decided to use my time to dream a little.

Anytime life felt like a bit too much at the moment, I projected my happiness forward and let myself dream big. I'd done this for years, something that an executive coach had once told me was a strength of mine, being strategic and future-oriented. She'd said that I always needed to have something to work towards, and she was right. While I really tried to be mindful of where I was at the moment, I got a great deal of joy from reaching for something in the future. Today, I needed that joy and the distraction.

I took out a sheet of graph paper from the stash I kept in the now super-organized register and walked outside. I knew I didn't want to lose my amazing gas station location with all its history and stories, so I wasn't going to move the shop. EVER. But that meant I had to strategize other means of expanding.

The men who owned the hardware store next door and I had casually discussed the parking lot between us. Neither of us had customers who used it much. It was just too small and awkward to turn around in what with the dead end at the guardrail by the alley. I wondered if they might be willing to let me buy it from the current owner and expand toward their store.

I took some quick measurements with the giant measuring tape my friend Woody had gifted me when we'd figured out the measurements for the new shelves he built for the shop. After measuring a few times to be sure I was understanding the space well, I realized I could have another twelve feet of shop space even if I left a small walkway between the hardware store and my shop. That seemed like plenty of new room.

Back inside at a café table, I started sketching the addition on the graph paper, putting in the now standard shelf sizes Woody and I had made for my book storage and imagining a dedicated event area at the back where authors could read and maybe I could have a musician play from time to time.

I got so excited that I took out my laptop, pulled up the county GIS map, and looked up the owner of the lot. All my energy fizzled out, though, when I saw the name of the owner of record: Edgar Levine.

The man was a bully, and I'd seen firsthand how he treated people he found beneath him. Plus, he was a suspect in

Margie's murder. I didn't know if I could handle negotiating with him. I felt deflated.

But just then, my dad knocked on the front door and waved. He still looked a little pale, and his smile was a bit forced. But I was glad to see him out and about. I jogged over and opened the door for him before giving him a big hug. He squeezed me tightly and said, "I was wondering if you needed help with anything."

I swallowed hard. My dad had never asked me that question before. Not to say he didn't help me. He did, all the time, but always at my request. This felt different, and given the sort of desperate look in his eyes, I needed to answer him.

In a flash of inspiration and dream-fueled hope, I said, "Feel like a big project?"

"Sure thing," he said with a bit more energy. "The bigger the better at this point."

We headed over to the café, where Rocky was just beginning her opening routine after coming in through the back door, and I asked if we could get two cinnamon rolls and two coffees with cream and sugar. Dad did not do vanilla latte despite my best efforts.

I showed him my piece of graph paper and told him about my idea to see if I could buy the lot next door. He immediately took the paper, studied it, made some financial projections for building costs, and then sat back. "Totally feasible if your mother and I invest," he said matter-of-factly.

I stared at him a long second. "What? You and mom would invest in my store?"

Dad smiled. "Of course we would, and honestly, while I don't know the specifics of your capital in-flow, I don't imagine it would be wise for you to go deeply into debt for this expansion."

I sighed. He was right. I had been thinking I'd take out a loan to cover the cost, but doing that would put me back in a tight financial position that I didn't want to be in again. I studied the numbers he'd tallied down the side, and the figure was a bit higher than I'd expected. Dad, however, knew numbers, if not construction specifically, and I imagined he was right.

My instinct was to tell my dad a big YES, but I was getting better and better about asking questions and sitting with decisions before leaping in. "So what would an investment from you two look like?"

Dad's smile widened into a grin. "That's my girl. Ask the good questions." He took a bite of his cinnamon roll and said, "Honestly, it would simply look like us giving you the capital to do the expansion and buy the lot next door. You'd retain full control of the store, but you'd simply have our backing on the financial end."

"And payback terms?" I asked.

"None. We would be investing your inheritance, so you'll just get it a little early." He patted my hands. "We want to support you in this wonderful thing you've done, Harvey, and I hope you'll consider letting us do that for you."

The tears were already spilling down my face, and all I could do was nod and then get up to hug my dad from behind. He reached up and squeezed my hand. "Now, how do we get started?"

I looked at the clock behind the café counter. Still a half-hour until we opened. "Well, I guess we start with seeing if we can buy the lot next door." My stomach sank. "But it's owned by Edgar Levine."

Dad pulled my arms from around his shoulders and pointed me back to my seat. "He's a total jerk, but I can handle him. I've managed worse."

I knew that was true. My dad had a soft heart, but he was a fierce business man. "But Dad, he's a suspect in the same murder that you are."

Dad nodded. "I know that, but does he know that?"

I shook my head. "I have no idea. Should I ask Tuck?"

"No, let's just leave this between us. I'll figure out the situation soon enough." He stood up. "Okay, I'm off to make a deal. Wish me luck."

I laughed. "Don't you need to talk to Mom first, be sure she's okay with your plan."

"Are you kidding? She's been trying to get me to make you this offer for six months. I'll let her know we're on when I pick her up in a few. She'll be thrilled, but not if I leave her out." He leaned over and gave me another quick hug. "Thanks for this, Harvey."

"Daddy," I said as I leaned into his chest. "Anytime I can use your money to build my dreams, I'm happy to oblige." I leaned back and grinned before he headed toward the front door.

Before I went over to open the shop, I ordered my usual vanilla latte from Rocky. "Did I just hear that you're going to expand the store?" She blushed. "Sorry for eavesdropping."

"You mean using your ears in a completely quiet space? Please. And yes, Mom and Dad are going to invest the money to let me expand." I did a little wiggle at the counter. "Between that and my date tonight, I don't know how I'm going to make it through the day."

"Did you say 'date?'" Marcus asked as he walked around the counter to give Rocky a kiss on the cheek and then smirk at me.

I blushed. "Yes, with Deputy Watson." I felt the flush on my cheeks grow darker and wished I had let my hair grow longer so I could use my curls to hide this streak of embarrassment that I seemed to be on.

"He's super cute," Rocky said before she glanced over at Marcus and said, "If you like blondes."

"I can dye this blonde for you, girl. Just say the word." Marcus ran a hand over his high top and laughed.

Rocky smiled. "No thank you. Let's leave the hair experimentation to me." She had recently had her hair crochet braided with long purple pieces woven in. It looked gorgeous, and when I saw her, I had vowed to myself to go back and have the blue streak put in my hair again.

"Actually, now that you mention it, if you don't mind, I might see if I can get a cut today. Keep my mind off things," I said to Marcus. "You up for me taking a long lunch break?"

"Of course, he is," Rocky answered for him. "And when you come back, I'll do your make-up for your date. Gotta look your best."

"It's just dinner at his house," I said.

"Woman," Marcus said. "That's the most serious kind of date of all." He looped his arm around my shoulders and led me and my latte back into the bookstore. "Let's get busy and keep your mind off things."

I waved at Rocky over my shoulder and let Marcus steer me to the counter. "Want to do the pick list right quick?"

I sighed but nodded. I hated pulling books to return, but with this expansion in the works and the reality of needing to keep a tight inventory to manage my bills, I knew I had to send some books back. I took comfort in the fact that Marcus hated the task as much as I did, and so we moved through the store, section by section, filling our library cart with book returns and saying thank you to all the books that we were sending back.

We were about a third of the way through the list when it was time to open, so Marcus unlocked the door and flipped on the neon sign before joining me in cooking to cull titles. Every few minutes, the bell over the door rang, and we kept an eye on customers as they browsed and when they needed to make a purchase.

By the time we finished the list, it was eleven-thirty, and I decided it was a good time to take a break and see about a haircut and color. "You good here?" I asked my assistant manager.

"More than good," Marcus said. "See you in a couple of hours." He waved and pushed our library cart to the back room.

The day was hot and humid, and I made my way quickly to the salon up the road. The stylist was new, and I was always a little nervous to let someone new cut my curly, coarse hair. But when I walked in and saw a gorgeous African American woman with beautifully coiffed curls that just reached her ears, much like mine, my nerves faded. She knew what she was doing.

Fortunately, she had time to see me, given that she was just building her business, and I sat down in her chair and explained that I only wanted a trim of my curls and then a bright blue streak in the front.

"So really bright, bright? Or just some bright?" she said with a smile.

"Really bright. Is that possible with my hair?" I asked.

"Totally, especially if I dye one of these silver streaks. Would that be okay?"

"I love it," I said and then let myself relax completely as she washed my hair, gave me an epic head massage, and then went to work.

By the time she was done, I felt more at ease than I had since the previous morning when I'd seen Margie's body at the post office, and even better, I looked great. The cut was subtle, but it let my curls be free. And the blue streak was brilliant but not too much. I looked like an edgy middle-aged woman, not a wanna-be teenager.

I tipped my new stylist and booked my next appointment for six weeks out, and then I fairly skipped back to the store. When I walked in both Marcus and Rocky wolf whistled at me, and I grinned. The day was getting better and better.

Marcus headed to the back room to box our returns, and I stayed on the floor answering questions and ringing up customers. So when Jared walked in around three, I was there to greet him. He stopped, admired my hair, and said, "It looks gorgeous. I love it."

I felt myself blush again, but for once, I didn't try to hide it. "Figured I'd spruce up for our date tonight."

His smile grew wider and then fell away. "You might want to change your mind about our date after I tell you what I need to tell you." He pointed toward the fiction section. "Can we sit?"

I caught Rocky's eye, and she walked quickly to the back to ask Marcus to staff the floor. Then, Jared and I sat down in the wingback chairs, and I took a deep breath. "Okay, hit me."

He leaned forward, frowned, and said, "Someone has come forward to say they saw your father at the post office yesterday morning."

My stomach plummeted into my feet. "What?! But that's not true."

"You're sure," he said, and while his words were soft and I could see the kindness in his eyes, my temper flared.

"I'm absolutely sure. My father did not kill Margie Riordan." All the blood was rushing out of my hands and feet, and I started to rub my fingers together. I was panicking, and I knew it, but I couldn't stop it.

"Breathe, Harvey. I didn't say someone said your father killed Margie. Someone just said they saw him there. Are you sure he couldn't have been there?" He reached over and put both of my hands in his.

Something about the gesture steadied me, and I caught my breath and took a minute. "I guess not. He could have been there to, you know, mail something." I forced myself to breathe as I felt my pulse quicken again.

Jared rubbed my fingers. "But you didn't see him?"

I pulled my hands away. "No, I didn't see him. Don't you think I would have told you if I did?"

He studied my face but didn't say anything.

I sighed. "That's why you're asking. You want to be sure I told Tuck everything?"

Jared reached over and took my hands again. "Yes. That's why I'm here before I talked to anyone else, even Tuck. I just got the report and came over." He rubbed his thumb over the knuckles on my right hand. "I'm glad to hear you didn't see him there, for many reasons."

For a few moments, I sat quietly, letting my pulse slow down and the warmth of Jared's hands sink in deep. If I hadn't been so anxious, I might have enjoyed the moment. But someone was setting my dad up, and I couldn't let that happen.

"I'm going to ask you something, and if you can answer, please do. If not, just tell me that, okay?" I held Jared's gaze a long minute. "Who said that?"

"I can't tell you that, Harvey, but can you trust me that I'm going to get to the bottom of this?" He didn't break eye contact when he spoke, and I felt a little peace reach the center of my chest.

"I think so. Thank you." He lifted our hands to his mouth and kissed my fingers before letting them go. "Does that mean we're still on for dinner, because if not, I'm going to have to eat a lot of lasagna? Alone. It's not a pretty thing to see a man with a casserole dish on the couch."

I smiled. "Yes, we're still on. See you in a little bit." We both stood, and he winked at me as he turned to head toward the cafe. I suddenly thought of something and jogged after him. "Wait, can I tell Dad?" My first instinct was to text him, but then I wondered if that would make things worse.

"I'm on my way to talk to him right now. He's meeting me here." He smiled. "I'll be gentle, Harvey."

I actually laughed at that. "Oh, don't be gentle. My dad appreciates shows of force." I grinned and walked to the register just as my dad walked in, waved, and headed toward the café to meet Jared.

It took every bit of willpower I had not to keep walking by and listening in, but for whatever reason, I did trust Jared, and I knew that my father would tell the truth, too. My father didn't kill that woman, I knew that. But it looked like someone wanted the police to think he did, and that I wasn't going to tolerate.

_____

5

As soon as Dad and Jared were done talking, Dad came over to find me where I was straightening the self-help section. I'd had to move as far away as I could from them to curb my eavesdropping temptation.

"Jared said he asked you if I was at the post office yesterday?" Dad said as he dropped into a chair nearby. "You told him you didn't see me."

"I did because that was the truth, but were you there?" I kept shelving, unsure whether I could handle the answer if I had to look Dad in the eye.

"I wasn't," he said. "I do go to the post office most mornings, though, but you know Mondays are my at-home days. Unfortunately, the only person who can vouch for my whereabouts is your mother."

"And spouses aren't always the best alibis," I finished.

"Right." He sighed and rubbed his hand over his jaw.

"The question is, I think, who lied about seeing you there. I know Jared probably didn't tell you, but maybe if we figure out who is setting you up, we'll find the killer and clear your name." I shoved a copy of *Atomic Habits* into place with too much force.

"Harvey," Dad's voice was full of caution. "We need to let the police do their job."

I sighed. "I know, but they need to focus on catching the killer. We can at least ask around and see who might have fingered you for this."

Dad grinned. "'Fingered me?' You have been watching far too much TV." He put his hands on top of his head. "Well, how about this? I have a meeting with Edgar Levine in," he looked at his watch, "fifteen minutes. I'll feel him out to see what he might know about the case."

I jumped up and down a little. "Perfect. But be careful, Daddy," I said, suddenly second-guessing our tactic here.

"Baby Girl, always." He kissed the top of my head and headed out the door. "I'll keep you and Jared posted. Have a great date."

The ridiculous blush of mine rose to my face again, and I started to ask how Dad knew about the date. But he was out the door before I had a chance. Had Jared told him? If so, why?

I didn't have much time to ponder that question, though, because as soon as I emerged from the shelves, Rocky corralled me into the back room for my make-up session. She got me seated and went to work. A little tinted sunscreen, some blush, a bit of shimmery eye shadow, something called a brow serum, mascara, and lip gloss had me ready to go. I looked nice – not overdone but like I cared how I looked. I was pleased, but apparently, Rocky wasn't done.

Then, she dipped a brush in a tiny cup of water she'd brought with her, stuck it in the darkest shade of her eyeshadow palette and lined the top of my eyes. As she held up the mirror from her bag to show me, I smiled. That little bit of eyeliner had made my green eyes more pronounced without making me look like I was going all Glow-Up smoky eye. Now, I looked like I was ready for a date.

"Thank you," I said as she refilled her make-up bag.

"Anytime, Harvey. It's nice to be pampered a bit sometimes." She picked up my hands then and rubbed the most amazing lotion into them. It smelled like oranges and honey, and I loved it. "A little scent but nothing extreme," she said.

I laughed. "That's wonderful," I said. "And I appreciate your restraint."

"Oh, I'll pull out all the stops on your first out-to-dinner date with Jared. For now, we take it easy." She squeezed my shoulder and led the way back out onto the floor.

For the second time that day, Marcus gave me a little cat call, and I swatted at him as I headed toward the front windows to grab my dogs for an evening walk. I had decided I'd leave them here at the store for my date and then pick them up after. Two extra bodies on a first date seemed like a little much.

But that meant the pups needed a stroll, and given that my shift at the store had just ended, I thought I could probably use the fresh air and time to clear my head, too. I waved to Marcus as I hooked up the dogs' leashes and headed out, this time in the opposite direction of Jared's house lest I appear too eager.

The dogs peed and sniffed their way down Main Street, and I greeted friends as we strolled. We stopped in to say hi to Cate and Henri at the art co-op, and the tourists and artists alike loaded the pups up with more attention than they'd need for days. Taco, of course, got the most snuggles because of those long ears, but a young woman with a gorgeous hibiscus tattooed on her neck took to Mayhem right away and snuggled her close as she sat on the floor for our entire visit.

When the pooches were fully loved up and Cate and Henri had given the big thumbs up to my hair and make-up, we headed back to the store. As we passed Chez Cuisine, I saw Max, the owner, through the window and gave him a wave. He smiled and held up one finger to ask me to wait. A few seconds later, he and Symeon joined us in front of the restaurant. "I was hoping to talk to you, Harvey," Max said.

I looked from him to Symeon and back. "About what?"

"Well, about Margie," he said quietly. "Do you know if they have made an arrest yet?"

Symeon's jaw tightened as he waited for my answer. Poor guy was so ready for this to be behind him.

"I don't think so," I said. "But Symeon, you don't have anything to worry about. Tuck and Jared will figure this out."

Symeon swallowed hard enough for me to see his Adam's apple bounce. "I know, but someone has been leaving mysterious messages on the restaurant voicemail."

I looked over at Max. "What kind of messages?"

"Ridiculous things," Max said, "just cryptic questions about whether or not I know who I have working for me and things like that."

I groaned. "Whoever killed Margie is working really hard to incriminate everyone else." I explained about someone lying to the police about my dad's whereabouts. "Have you told the police about the phone calls?"

"Not yet," Symeon said. "I wasn't sure what they'd think."

Max shook his head. "We need to tell them, Sy. Withholding this kind of information only makes you look more guilty."

I nodded. "I understand your hesitation, but Max is right."

"Alright," Symeon said with a groan. "If it's okay with you, I'll go the station now to tell them."

"Actually, let's have Tuck come here. That way, he can hear the messages themselves," Max said.

"And Max can be with you," I added.

Max smiled. "Exactly."

I wished the men the best and asked for an update tomorrow, but then I hurried back to the store, deposited the now exhausted dogs on their beds, and grabbed my purse. It was time for my date.

THE WALK OVER WAS LOVELY, if still a bit humid, and I tried to focus on the way the light turned golden against the trees at this time of day and year. The appreciation of the way sunshine changed was a skill I had been learning to cultivate actively on my daily walks. Everything look different, even on the same path, depending on the time and season. I wasn't a visual artist, but I could definitely see how a painter could appreciate the various ways light created beauty.

By the time I reached Jared's house, I felt pretty good, not distracted, and ready for a fun night. And when I saw that he had hung Edison bulbs across the front of his porch and set up a lovely table in the corner under his blooming magnolia tree, I was even more excited. Fans turned on both sides of the wrap-around porch, and when I walked up the stairs, the gentle breeze cooled the air just enough to make it very comfortable.

Before I could ring the bell, Jared opened the door and smiled. "You look gorgeous," he said and kissed my cheek before inviting me in. "Would you like a tour?"

I glanced up at the gorgeous wooden banister leading to the upstairs and said, "Yes, definitely. This is beautiful." I ran my hand along the wooden spindles. "Original?"

"Fortunately, yes." He walked through a wide doorway to the left, and as I followed, I saw it was a beautiful pocket door. "Most of the other wood was painted, so I've been slowly stripping all the woodwork back to the original oak. It's a shame someone covered that up."

I laughed. "You sound like the Rehab Addict," I said remembering the opening to her show.

"She's a genius if a bit too peppy for my taste," he said. I looked around at the living room, which featured a fireplace, the antique mantel Jared had mentioned hunting for, and a beautiful tufted sectional in a lovely hunter green. I had to resist the temptation to sit down and stretch out my feet. It looked so comfortable.

Through the door at the back of the living room, I could see where most of the renovation had happened. "Did you take out a wall here?" I asked as we crossed into an open dining room–kitchen combination.

"Yep. I didn't want an entire open floor plan, but I liked the idea of having the dining room and kitchen together." The décor was another blend of contemporary and period with tall cabinets in white on the uppers and dark gray on the lowers. The counters were soapstone, and I let my hand rest on their cool surface. He took the bottle of white wine from me and slid it into the freezer.

"It's gorgeous, and a real chef's kitchen," I noted as I pointed at the two ovens in the wall and the gas cooktop in the center island. "Plenty of workspace."

He nodded. "Do you cook?"

I smiled. "I do, but not as much as I'd like because of my work hours. I enjoy it though." I took a deep breath. "Something smells heavenly."

"My grandmother's recipe. For a Finn, she was strikingly good with Italian food," he said as he opened the door to the lower oven and pulled out a beautiful blue Le Creuset casserole dish full of steaming cheese and tomato sauce. As he set it on the counter, he said, "Just enough time to finish the tour while it cools and the garlic bread finishes up."

We made our way through a second door at the other side of the kitchen and stepped back into the hallway by the stairs. "There's a half bath under the staircase," he said without stopping and then moved to the end of the staircase. "Here's my study," he said as he swung open a gorgeous, heavy door.

As soon as I stepped inside, I gasped. The entire room was

lined with bookshelves, and each shelf was full. I walked over to one shelf and began to read the titles. The first shelf I studied held a whole collection of books on walking including *Beneath My Feet: Writers On Walking* and one of my favorites, *Wanderlust* by Rebecca Solnit. I smiled as I ran my fingers down its spine and moved on.

His books were all arranged categorically, so he had shelves for books on foodways, one for a classic sci-fi collection, several of fantasy novels, and a huge ancient history collection that included titles about Ancient Greece, early Babylon, and pre-Columbian North America. When I took *1491* by Charles Mann off the shelf, Jared walked over and said, "Such a good book. Have you read it?"

I shook my head as I scanned the back cover. "Should I?"

"If you like to read about Native American cultures, definitely. It's so good. Not a quick read but a good one." He smiled at me. "Want to borrow it?"

I laughed. "You know, people offer to let me borrow books all the time, but I know this bookstore owner. She gets me a good deal when I order them."

"Totally. Well, maybe she can order some titles I've been looking for?" he said with a grin.

"She absolutely can, and if this date goes well, I'll put in a good word for you so you can get the friends and family discount." I leaned over and kissed his cheek and then went through the final door in the room, hoping I wasn't being too forward . . . in any way.

There, I found a quiet little sitting room with comfortable chairs, several reading lights, and a puzzle table in the middle. I couldn't resist sitting down at the table and picking up a piece to see if I could fit it into the puzzle of what looked to be Angkor Wat. When I slipped one in, I double-tapped the piece and stood up. "Now, I feel better. "

"You like puzzles?" Jared said with one eyebrow raised.

"Love them but don't do them much because my cat Aslan is notorious for batting the pieces around the room." I grinned at my date and found him studying me.

"I like you, Harvey Beckett," he said quietly and took my hand to lead me to the porch, where he poured me a glass of water and said, "I'll be right back with your wine."

I smiled and resisted the urge to offer to help. "Sometimes it's good to be a little pampered," Rocky had said, and I decided I was going to let myself believe that.

A few moments later, Jared came out with two glasses of wine and salad for each of us. The greens were a mix of iceberg lettuce, spinach, and arugula tossed in a light vinaigrette with cherry tomatoes and baby corn. It was delicious and just the right thing to eat before heavy pasta.

When our salads were done, Jared brought out the casserole dish and set it between us with a huge spoon projecting from the side. "I figured we might just want to decide our own portions."

"Good plan," I said as I cut myself a huge piece and set it on the pristine white plate before me. "I may also need seconds."

Jared laughed. "I like a woman who appreciates food."

"I am that woman," I said as a lifted the first forkful to my lips and took a bite. It was delicious – flavorful and warm, filled with cheese, spinach, and al dente pasta. "Man, you may never get rid of me if you keep this up."

"I think I could handle that," Jared said as pink tinted his cheeks.

We ate quietly for a few minutes and then I asked Jared about the rest of the plans for his house. "More big reno to do or just finishing touches?"

He told me about his plan to remodel the upstairs bathroom into something a little more modern but said that was the last major thing. "Then, it's just decorating. I'm finding I really like that part."

"Good on you for that," I said as I ate my last bite of pasta. "I have no eye for décor. Your house is gorgeous, though. I like what you've done."

He smiled. "Seconds?" he said as he helped himself to a small second piece of lasagna.

I patted my stomach and said, "Well, that depends on whether or not those cannoli were just an empty promise."

"Definitely not. I can't say I made those, though. There's this baker in Annapolis that sells the best ones I've ever had. I stopped over this morning and got some."

"This morning?" I said as I did take a second portion of garlic bread. I couldn't resist the butter and garlic combo. "Didn't you work today?"

He grinned. "I'm an early riser, so I did my run over there and grabbed the cannoli before I headed back for my shift."

"Early? It sounds like you were up before dawn." I tried to remember the last time I'd seen the sunrise. I was a morning person, but morning for me started about seven.

"Five every morning. I like to get some things done early on." He shrugged. "What does your day usually look like?" he asked as he began to clear our plates.

I picked up the casserole and bread platter and followed him to the kitchen. "I get up early, or at least I thought it was early, and depending on whether I open the store or not, I have a good breakfast, do a little reading, putter in the garden, and then head in. Usually, Mart and I hang out in the evenings and watch movies or play with the dogs. Pretty laid-back life, really."

"That sounds great. Do you like to get out on the water?" he asked as he scraped our plates into a compost bucket on the table and slid the dishes into the dishwasher. A man who composts – be still my heart.

"I do like the water," I said when I could pry my mind away from the fact that this guy cared about the environment. "I don't get out as much as I'd like, but my friends Stephen and Walter just bought a party boat. So I expect we'll be gathering out there more often now."

"That's awesome. And also a sure sign of middle age when the party boat is the choice instead of the speed boat," he said with a chuckle. "I was looking at one myself."

I laughed. "Yep, we're all for seats while we sip our fancy cocktails." I glanced out the back window. "Is that your garden?" A series of raised beds stretched out beyond the window, and in each, I could see plants rising up, verdant and tall.

"Want to see it?" he asked as he took my hand again. "It's my hobby."

"Cooking. Gardening. Running. Home repair. Do you sleep?" I felt myself getting a little nervous that he was going to tell me he only rested for about four hours a night, and I was going to have to end this before it really got started because I needed my eight, sometimes nine hours, and didn't think I could be with someone who never slept.

"Oh my yes, at least eight hours a night. I just stay busy when I'm awake. Unless, of course, I'm catching up on my vampire shows." He winked at me and opened the back door.

As we walked through the garden hand in hand, he told me about what plants he grew to eat – tomatoes, cucumbers, peas, sweet corn, and beans – and which he grew just because he loved them – burgundy okra, ornamental corn, and a variety of flowers. "I try squash every year, and every year the squash bugs destroy my crop. One year, I'll get those little jerks in time," he said.

We wandered through his side yard, and I admired the house – two stories with what looked like an attic above. The windows were mullioned, a term I had learned by reading Victorian ghost stories, and the foundation looked to be made from field stone. It was a gorgeous home, and I could see that Jared's TLC was improving it day by day.

When we reached the front porch, he poured another glass of wine for each of us and asked if I wanted to see the upstairs. I nodded enthusiastically and then followed him, wine in hand, up the stairs. To the left was the bathroom he had mentioned remodeling, and while it was a quaint 1950s bath, I could see why he wanted it updated. Mint green tile is just not that fashionable these days, and I wasn't even sure I could fit under that low shower head.

To the right were two bedrooms, each with a queen-sized bed, night stands, and a dresser, all antiques as best I could tell. "Do you like to have house guests?" I asked.

"Sometimes, although I also usually like to see them leave," he said with a smile. "My parents and sister come some, and I want them to feel comfortable when they're here." He pointed toward the end of the hall. "That's my room. If it doesn't feel weird, I'd like to show it to you."

I shook my head. "Not weird at all. I need to see if you have a Damon-style bed in the middle of the room after all."

He threw back his head and laughed. "Hardly." When he opened the door, I saw a simple, sleigh bed with a white down-filled bedspread on it and two matching night tables. It was simple and masculine but also complete. So many men slept on bare mattresses, if the photos from the dating sites I'd tried out were accurate, sometimes without box springs, and I was pleased to see he had an actual bedroom set. I wanted to be with a grown-up, not a man-boy. I was pleased to see this man was fully grown.

We made our way back down the stairs to the porch and sat at the table in companionable silence for a few minutes. But then, my sweet tooth took over and said, "Have I been polite and patient enough that I won't seem rude to say I'm dying for a cannoli?"

Jared grinned. "I thought you'd never ask." He stepped back inside, and I took a deep breath of the cooling summer air. The sky was turning that shade of lavender that gets such a bad rap because of its association with prissy little girls, and I felt a little zip of excitement at the idea of watching the sunset with Jared. When he came back out, he held a plate with three cannoli in one hand and a single white candle on a silver holder in the other. "A little candlelight isn't too much is it?"

I smiled. "Not at all," I said as I stood, took the candle and set it in the middle of the table before pulling his chair over next to mine so that we could both see the sun as it dropped below the trees.

"I like this idea," he said and sat down next to me, taking my hand without a moments' hesitation. "A sunset dessert is just about perfect."

I held back the "Like you" that I wanted to whisper into the air and just smiled. This night was just about as perfect as it got.

We watched the sun go down, and then, I knew it was time for me to go. I had the feeling we could have enjoyed each other's company for many hours more, but we were both going to have to be up early, some of us earlier than others – five a.m. egads! – and I didn't want to stay so long that it began to feel awkward.

When I said it was time for me to go, Jared didn't protest. He simply walked me to the porch steps and said, "This was a wonderful night, Harvey. Thank you for sharing it with me." Then he leaned over and kissed me softly just for a second on the lips.

I once against resisted my urges and didn't grab his flannel shirt and pull him in for more. Instead, I turned and walked off the porch and headed toward Main Street.

"Harvey?" Jared called. "Did you walk here?"

I looked back over my shoulder. "Yes. From the store. I'm

going there now to get the dogs and head home." I smiled. "I walk most everywhere in town."

A crease formed in his brow. "I would feel better if I walked you to the store. Would that be okay?"

I studied him for a second and then nodded. "Sure." When he joined me and took my hand again, I smiled but then said, "Do you think it's never safe for a woman to walk alone, or is something in particular worrying you?"

He glanced over at me. "Let's just say that my job affords me the knowledge about a lot of nefarious things. Tonight, those nefarious things feel close, and I don't want anything to happen to you."

I squeezed his fingers and let him walk me to the door of the store. I opened it, captured the dogs who bounded toward me, and leashed them up. "I'm all set. These two are fearsome guard dogs if they need to be."

Jared knelt down and scratched their ears before whispering between their heads, "You bark loud and clear if you need help, okay?"

The dogs panted and seemed to nod, and Jared stood and smiled. "A bonus of getting to escort you is that, if you don't mind, I will steal another of these." He looked down at my lips.

"I don't mind at all," I said as he leaned forward and gave me another, slightly longer kiss on the lips before I set the alarm, and we walked the block to his street and parted ways.

6

The next morning at six-fifteen I was awakened by a text. I rolled over, thinking (hoping) it might be Jared and instead found it was my father. "I didn't want to disrupt your date, but I have good news. Meet you at the store at eight?"

I rubbed the sleep from my eyes and sat up. "Okay," I said although that was a full four hours before I was due to be there. Today was my day to close, and I had been looking forward to a leisurely morning. Dad, though, wasn't one to text, period, much less to say he had good news. Besides, maybe I could wander around town and see some folks after I talked to Dad. I hadn't been over to the maritime museum in a while, and Lucas had said they had a new exhibit about African American boatmen up.

After I extricated my cat, Aslan, from her hovel between my legs, I stood, stretched, and headed for the shower. The hot water felt great, just the thing I needed after a night of sleeping so hard that I had barely moved.

When I'd gotten home last night, Mart and Symeon had been playing gin rummy in the living room and had wanted all the details. I indulged their curiosity and described dinner and Jared's house, but I left out the sunset and the two kisses because, well, I wanted to keep some things for myself. Then, I'd joined in a game that had turned into three and before I knew it, the clock said eleven, and I was almost asleep on the coffee table.

I hadn't been worried about the late night when I thought I could sleep until at least seven, but I was awake early now, which meant my caffeine need was great. I quickly pressed a pot in the French press Mart had given me recently when she'd decided I needed to cut back on my caffeine habit and not drink an entire eight-cup pot by myself before going to work and drinking, well, more. She had been right, and the French press made two perfect cups, which I took the time to savor with my latest read, *This Savage Song.*

I was a huge Victoria/V.E. Schwab fan, and this duology was proving to be great, too. Monsters who aren't all monsters, a girl with something to prove, the possibility of romance. It was all YA fantasy could be, and I loved it.

At seven-forty-five, after only getting up to let the dogs out and feed them, I put away the book reluctantly, gave Aslan a little tuna as an apology for leaving her early, and leashed up the dogs. The day was already getting warm, but for once, the humidity didn't bother me, much. I was still on a high from my date with Jared, and whatever good news Dad had was going to buoy my spirits I was sure.

The text from Jared as I entered town didn't hurt either. All it said was "Thank you for last night, and enjoy your walk to work," but the thoughtfulness made me feel all warm and fuzzy until the honk of a car horn sent my heart racing. I looked over to see Jared driving by in his cruiser, clearly on his way in to work himself. So he had seen me walking, not just remembered I did. I smiled even more.

Dad was already waiting when I got to the store, and I

unlocked the door, turned off the alarm, and led him to the café. Coffee wasn't ready yet, but I saw two scones in the case that would be perfect and plated them for us before sitting down.

"So what's this good news that couldn't wait?" I asked as I took a bite of my honey orange scone.

"I got the lot," he said.

I coughed and spewed scone all over the table and his arms. "You what?"

"The parking lot. I bought it last night." His grin showed most of his back molars.

"Already? How? I thought it took days to do real estate transactions." I was trying to wrap my head around the idea that my dream was about to get even better, but I couldn't get past the logistics.

"Well, we haven't done the purchase yet, but Levine signed a contract with me last night, and we'll do the exchange of title later today. The lot is yours, Harvey, to do with as you wish." He patted my hand as it rested on the table.

"Just like that," I asked. "Levine didn't resist at all?"

"Well, I wouldn't say that," Dad said as he looked down at the table, "I had to do a little finagling."

"What kind of finagling?" I asked.

"You really want to know?" he asked as he looked at me.

"I do. I probably need to know just in case, right?"

"There shouldn't be any problems going forward, Harvey, but it certainly wouldn't hurt for you to be up to speed." He took a bite of his scone, swallowed, and said. "Well, the town had been trying to buy the lot for a few years. They wanted to put a community garden in there, but Levine was charging an extortionist's price for the lot. The town just couldn't swing it."

I paled. "You didn't pay too much did you, Daddy?" This time I grabbed his hand.

He smiled. "Would I do that, Baby Girl?"

I relaxed. My dad had never overpaid for a piece of real estate. In fact, if he paid market value, he considered that over-paying. I should have known. "So how did you manage it?"

"For Levine, this is all about ego, so I played to his. Before I met with him, I asked the mayor if it would be possible to locate the garden elsewhere, contingent on the fact that I could find a suitable lot near downtown. They didn't see any problem with that, and I quickly secured a small lot, on their behalf, just on the backside of the art co-op. Cate was happy to sell it at a good price, and the town was happy to buy." He smiled at his ingenious real estate acumen, and I couldn't blame him.

"So you took Levin's potential buyer away?" I said with a grin. "What did he say to that?"

"Well, he agreed to my price on one condition." He rolled his eyes. "We have to call the garden the Edgar Levine garden."

"Seriously?! The dude is petty enough to want a bunch of unweeded tomatoes and rampant bean plants to be named in his honor." I'd seen enough community gardens back in San Francisco to know that people started out strong on the gardening front but then fizzled off as the heat rose. Heck, I knew that from my own garden patch.

"He does. And I agreed. It's a small price to pay for the garden and for your dream." He stood up and pulled me to my feet. "So now, we just need a contractor."

I grinned. "Oh, I know just the men for that job," I said and took out my phone.

Within minutes, I had arranged for Dad to meet with both Walter, whose experience as a building contractor would be invaluable, and Woody, the man who knew this building better than I did. In fact, they were coming over shortly. Retirement had its benefits – like a completely open schedule.

While we waited, Dad did some more sketches on my graph paper, and I helped Marcus with the opening tasks. Of course, since he'd closed the night before, the store was immaculate.

We did, however, have a few sparse spots on the front shelves, probably as a result of Marcus's talent for hand-selling titles. The man had a real knack for this work.

Soon enough, the shelves and tables were full again, the smell of coffee was wafting through the air, and Marcus had the door unlocked. The small group of morning regulars funneled their way in, many to the café, a couple to the books they had been reading slowly over the past few days, and two to me, where I stood waiting for them beside the café entrance.

Walter and his husband, Stephen, had come East from San Francisco just after I did, wanting to slow down their pace of life and able to take good advantage of the ridiculous real estate market out West to buy a gorgeous waterfront place here after selling their apartment in San Francisco. Now, I hugged my dear friend and thanked him for coming.

Then, I gave my other special customer, Woody, a huge hug. He had done so many projects for me around the store, not just building bookshelves but also burning our sign above the front door and building planter boxes that got daily compliments for the front windows. I felt his scraggly gray beard brush my face as I pulled away and stared at his twinkling blue eyes. He always reminded me of a sort of woodsman-like Santa, especially with the perpetual blush on his cheeks. "You smell amazing," I said as I let go and turned toward the café.

"Been making a cedar chest." He gently shook a little sawdust from his beard into his hand. "Forgot to clean up, I was so excited to hear this plan of yours."

I grinned. "Well, then, let's talk."

Dad had already pulled two tables together, laid out a sort of rudimentary blueprint made from my graph paper and scotch tape, and put a carafe of coffee on the windowsill nearby. He was ready to work, and I found my excitement level ticking up another notch.

We all sat down after handshakes between the men, and

Dad didn't waste any time. "Gentlemen, if you're willing, I'd like to hire you to expand Harvey's bookstore."

Walter and Woody looked at me and then at my dad. For a split second, I thought they might ask some good questions, get some specs, and say they'd consider it, which of course would be the reasonable response. But then, they both said, in unison, "Definitely."

"When do we start?" Walter asked.

Dad grinned. "We haven't yet closed on the lot next door, but as soon as that's finalized, this afternoon, we can begin breaking ground."

"Perfect," Woody said before turning to Walter. "That is if you don't mind having an old woodworker who has to take frequent breaks on your crew."

"Mind? I wouldn't have it any other way," Walter said as he set a hand on Woody's shoulder. "I'm hoping you'll be my foreman."

A smile broke across Woody's face, and warmth spread through my chest. My friends continued to amaze me with their generosity toward me and each other.

For the next hour, the men talked through the plan, stopping every few minutes to ask me about what features I wanted in the addition. I told them I wanted as much light as possible without sacrificing the nature of the original building. I also wanted that reading/performance space and plenty of new shelving. Then, I paused, braced myself, and said, "Also, a dog nook with built-in water bowls." My dad thought my obsession with my dogs was a little extreme, and I wondered what he would say.

But he didn't even pause in his note-taking, and before I could say anything further, Walter had sketched in a platform by a window and even marked out a corner with raised water bowls in their own stand. If I hadn't already felt like I might burst with joy, I'm sure my heart would have filled even more.

"Thank you," I whispered, and Walter put his hand on mine and squeezed before going back to his notes about supplies and sub-contractors.

As the conversation got more and more technical and my store got more and more busy, I excused myself and headed back to do the job I knew how to do best. A small, thin woman with light freckles on her nose and a thick braid of blonde hair down her back stood in the fiction section, and as usual, I tried to guess what she was looking for as I approached. If I went with the stereotype, she might have been searching for historical fiction, maybe some Jane Austen, but years of reading and talking about books, told me that people usually defied stereotypes when it came to books.

"Can I help you find something?" I said with a smile as I joined her by the Ls.

"Actually yes. I loved *Music for Torching*, and I'd like to read something like that again. Any suggestions?"

I thought of A.M. Homes' beautiful but striking novel about a wife who steps way out of her normal day-to-day to explore life and smiled. This customer was not the stereotype at all. "Are you looking for literary? Racy? Domestic?"

A grin spread across her face. "A little racy but also very literary. I'm not bothered by disturbing content or stories that make me think as long as the writing is gorgeous, too."

"Great," I said as I walked along the shelves. "This one isn't racy, but it is beautiful and hard in the most human way." I handed her a copy of *The Weight of Memory* by Shawn Smucker as I kept scanning the shelves. "And this one skews a bit more toward horror," I looked to see if that bothered her, but when she didn't even blink, I said, "but it's gorgeous and so creepy because of how real it feels."

She looked at the cover of *The Book of Accidents* and said, "These both look perfect. Thank you." We wandered toward the register, and she looked around with a smile as I rang up her purchases. I made a note to ask Marcus's mom, who writes our monthly newsletter, to do a recommendation list for edgy and literary books just with this reader in mind. It would be a great addition to the more light and summery fare we usually discussed in August.

As the customer left, Smucker's book already open in her hands, I smiled. I loved my job.

That smile faded quickly when Edgar Levine blustered in, stormed over to me at the register and said, "How dare you?"

Given that this was the second time someone had shouted at me at my own store's register in three days, I was a little raw and felt tears spring to my eyes. I held them back, though, and said, "Can I help you, Mr. Levine?"

My quiet tone must have caught him off-guard because he hesitated, but then came back full-force. "You told the police I killed that woman at the post office." His voice echoed throughout the store, and I felt a shiver of rage scurrying up my spine as customers turned to stare.

"Mr. Levine, you will lower your voice or I will have to ask you to leave?" I hissed and refused to remember how my mother had said the exact same thing in the exact same spot. "I did not tell the police any such thing. I did tell them about the very loud and inappropriate phone conversation you had here where you claimed that your assistant had sabotaged your plans for an unethical land grab and the way you were implying that Postmistress Riordan had something to do with that."

Clearly, Levin had underestimated both my eavesdropping prowess and my ability to determine the context of a one-sided conversation because he took a step back.

At that moment, I felt someone take my arm from behind and another body step to my other side. Dad and Walter had joined me, and Woody was coming around the counter toward

Levine. "Want me to take this gentleman outside?" Woody asked as he stared up at the much larger man.

I knew Woody was just saying he'd walk him to the door, but for a moment I smiled as at the image of Woody getting ready to give someone a beating.

"Mr. Levine, you would do well to mind your words, sir," my dad said quietly but with a level of menace I had never heard in his voice before. "I will see you at three to finish our business."

Summarily dismissed and clearly outmatched, Levine huffed and then stomped back out the door as I let myself slump onto my daddy's arm. "That man needs anger management classes," I said and then took a deep breath and stood up. "Thank you." I looked at all three men, and they simply smiled and went back to their work.

I, however, found I wanted some fresh air, so after checking in with Marcus, I leashed up the dogs and headed out for a walk. I resisted the urge to stroll casually passed Jared's place only because I knew he was at work and headed, instead, toward the art co-op. That would, of course, take me just in front of the police station. I was not subtle, that was for sure.

But when I walked by the station, I didn't see anyone but the dispatcher at the front desk and kept on moving even as a small wave of disappointment washed over me. As my dogs tugged me toward the co-op, I forced myself to let my down feelings go. We'd had a great night. I didn't need to force things. They were developing nicely already.

As we approached the building where Cate and her fellow artists had their studios, the dogs began to pull hard, and when the door opened and Cate and her Scottish Terrier, Sasquatch, walked out, I laughed. Taco and Mayhem were thrilled to see one of their best doggy friends.

And I was equally happy to see one of my people ones. "Care to join the sniff and pee brigade?" I asked with a grin.

"As long as we don't have to sniff or pee, I'm in," Cate chuckled. "Just getting some air?"

"Yeah, it's been an intense morning at the shop. I needed a little break." I told her about the plans to expand, about how fast they were moving, and about how that was both thrilling and terrifying. Then I said, "And then Edgar Levine came in and screamed at me."

"That man," Cate growled. "Did you know that he once took one of our painters to task for not using the *exact* shade of magenta he imagined when he commissioned the piece?"

"I could name three hundred things wrong with that idea including that he was asking for a piece of art not an interior design."

"Exactly." Cate shook her head as we walked up the street. "The painter took his check, which she had yet to cash, out of her desk, handed it to him, and told him never to speak to her again."

"That's amazing," I said.

"I had the privilege of seeing him leave the co-op, and I think his face was about the shade of magenta he had requested." She cackled with glee as she stopped to pick up Sasquatch's business. "It was amazing."

I laughed as we turned the corner to walk up the other side of the block. As we passed in front of Elle's shop, she tapped on the window and waved us inside. "Have time?" I asked Cate.

"Definitely," she said as she slipped Sasquatch's lease around the maple tree by the road and watched me do the same with my two pups. All three of them tucked their heads into the large water bowl Elle kept outside and then stretched out like sunbeams radiating from the tree trunk. They had all possible directions for petting monitored.

Inside Elle's lovely store, I took a deep breath. The entire space smelled like chrysanthemums and basil, and while I had never imagined that combination, it was wonderful. On the rustic wooden shelves by the front windows, she had crates of the produce she grew and some she sold on behalf of local farmers – cantaloupes, cucumbers, all manner of tomatoes. Just looking at the selection made me so hungry.

At the back of the storefront, Elle was working on a lovely small arrangement of zinnias and yarrow, all pinks and oranges and golds that looked like the epitome of summer. The vase was a simple flared one, but the sides were etched with small stems that both accented and softened the living stems in the water behind them. "That vase is amazing," I said.

"Isn't it?" Elle replied as she tucked a bit of cosmos greenery in amongst the blooms. "Thanks for putting me on to the artist, Cate."

"Wait, she's a local artist? Is she at the co-op?" I asked.

"She is . . . but in a special space at the back of the building that we don't let visitors go into because of, well, the glass fragments flying through the air. It has a special ventilation system. We keep our kilns in there, and she works in one corner." Cate picked up one of the arrangements that Elle had already finished. "Your flowers look amazing in these. Has she seen them?"

Elle smiled. "I sent her a few pictures. I'm hoping they will help her garner a few more customers, especially since she can't have an open studio."

"I'll buy some. Maybe we can use these in the shop for your flowers, Elle? Donate the ones we've been using?" I asked.

"Actually, we're going to be doing a recycling campaign to get this artist and others material for their work. So we could use your old vases, and she could melt them down for new projects?" Cate said.

"Yes, let's do that!" I said as I studied one of the still empty vases. "You'll put me in touch about buying some for the shop," I asked Cate as my mind began to turn on a new project. "And maybe we can help with your recycling campaign?"

Elle laughed. "Leave it to you, Harvey, to go from a casual walk with the dogs to a full-on philanthropic enterprise in five minutes flat."

I blushed. I had done a fair share of fundraisers in my time here, a fact that my mother loved now that fundraising wasn't my career of choice. I just loved helping people, and while I didn't have the time or much money to give, I did have a bit of influence and a lot of energy, most days at least. "You guys know I love this stuff."

This time both Cate and Elle smiled. "We do, so let's do it. The three of us can pull something together," Cate said.

"Perfect, and if the artists can't use the items we get, we can donate them to Habitat for Humanity," Elle added.

"Ooh, this is exciting," I said and wiggled a little. "Get together tonight and plan? Our house at seven-thirty?"

We spent a few minutes sketching out what everyone would bring to eat for our Girls Gone Recycling night, and then I took the dogs and headed back to the shop as Cate returned to the co-op. As I made my way back to the store, I sort of skipped. I'd had a great date, my shop was getting expanded, and I was part of a great project to help both our earth and local artists. It was a good day. Now, if we could just clear my dad and Symeon of this murder, all would be right in the world.

7

Blessedly, the afternoon went smoothly and without any excitement at the store. And when I got a sweet text that said, "Thank you for last night. Let's do it again soon," from Jared, I had to really suppress my smile so as not to terrify the teenage boy who was looking for great books that were scary. I didn't think he'd scare easily, but I remembered how adults seemed both so alluring and dangerous when I was his age.

Fortunately, I was able to put him on to V. C. Andrews Flowers In the Attic books, and when I said they were "vintage," he and his faux glasses and skinny jeans were thrilled.

I waited until I had rung him up before I texted Jared back and said, "Friday, my place?" Mart was going out of town for the night to coordinate some massive wine tasting event in DC, and I thought it might be nice to show Jared where I lived. Plus, I wasn't sure I was ready to have the entire town watch our date at one of our three restaurants.

His response was immediate. "Five-thirty? This time I'll bring the wine."

I confirmed and then spent the rest of the afternoon

straightening shelves while I hummed the same refrain from Over The Rhine's song "Drunkard's Prayer" again and again. After a while, I was even annoying to myself, but I couldn't stop. I was happy. Really happy.

And that night, when Cate showed up with a tofu stir-fry, Elle an amazing Cobb salad, and Mart with some of her winery's incredible Chardonnay, I was in hog heaven. Good friends, good food, a good cause.

As we gathered around the table, Cate told us about what materials her artists could use. Art supplies – paints, canvases, brushes, clay, and more – were obvious, but they also needed paper that was both used and new, yarn, old clothing that would be pulped or cut for various projects, and intact glass objects like my vases.

With our initial goal plan, we decided we really wanted to do more, so we decided to expand to include building supplies, too. Elle had already reached out to the nearby Habitat for Humanity store, and they were happy to come pick up items we gathered for them. So we could advertise that we were taking donations of old building supplies, doors, windows, and even furniture.

Mart used her considerable skills with graphic design to make up some flyers and images we could use to advertise, and we each used our phones to begin posting immediately to social media. Since we wanted to maximize our time and efforts as well as take advantage of the empty space in the parking lot my dad had just closed on this afternoon – his excited text confirmed that everything was finalized – we decided to schedule the recycling drive for this coming Saturday. We'd pulled off bigger feats in less time, and I loved the time pressure of getting something done.

Plus, I wanted to use the event to announce the expansion of All Booked Up, and I thought this was a great opportunity. A quick text to Walter confirmed that we could do some sort of ceremonial "brick breaking" that day, and I was happy with that, even if I secretly hoped we might actually start work that day, too. I wasn't exactly what you would call a patient person when it came to things that got me excited.

Once our social media posts were up, I texted all our friends and asked them to help us spread the word. As usual, they were all in, especially Mom, who immediately said she'd contact the local nonprofits and ask them to spread the word as well as contact the paper and local news stations with a press release.

By the time, Cate and Elle had helped me clean up, Galen had already shared the Recycle for Art and Home event to his Instagram, all our friends had offered to come help us that day as well as promote the event, and Mom had two press interviews for Cate lined up for tomorrow. We were all thrilled and exhausted as we said goodbye, and Mart and I only made it through one episode of the new *The Originals* before hitting the hay.

I did, however, decide to send Jared one last text before bed just to say I was looking forward to Friday. His reply was immediate and included a kissing heart emoji. I'm pretty sure I fell asleep with a smile on my face.

THE NEXT MORNING, I was still smiling as I made my morning coffee, fried up some egg whites and home-grown spinach for Mart and me, and headed off with two well-fed and well-rested pups to open the store. I practically skipped as I walked up to Main Street, but when I saw the small crowd and two police cruisers in front of my door, my skip turned into a sprint and my smile fell away.

Jared caught my arm as I tried to run by him, and when he pulled me to face him, I resisted, even though at a second's glance, I could see the concern on his face. "Harvey, wait."

The heaviness in his words was the only thing that stopped

me from breaking free and running over to see what exactly had everyone staring. But I did stop and look at him. "What happened?!"

"Your store has been vandalized. Tuck is taking pictures, and then, I will help you clean up." He held my gaze. "We're on this, Harvey."

I stared at him for a minute, and then took a deep breath as he let me turn around. Scrawled across the beautiful sign Woody had made me was the word, "Hypocrite" in blue spray paint.

I gasped and put my hand to my mouth as the tears slid down my cheeks. I wasn't worried about being called names, but my sign, all Woody's hard work – it was ruined.

Jared took my hand. "Woody is on his way. He thinks he can fix it."

I looked over at the man beside me. "Really?"

Jared nodded. "Really." He squeezed my fingers. "I'm going to get folks to move on. Meet you inside in a few minutes?"

I tried to smile but just nodded, and then the dogs and I stepped around Tuck, who nodded and kept photographing the front of my store, and went inside. I was the first one to arrive, and so I took my time as I did the morning routine and let my nerves settle.

As usual, I found my anxiety easing as I made my way among the books. My fingers slid over the spines, and the scent of paper and coffee soothed my spirit. By the time I had visited every section of titles and straightened the few books I'd missed in my rounds the night before, I was feeling much better.

And when Tuck and Jared knocked on the door, I was actually able to smile genuinely and roll my eyes as I said, "I promise. I have literally done nothing beyond talk with my friends about Margie's murder." In the past, I had been a bit too involved in Tuck's investigations, but I had really learned my lesson and was leaving all the sleuthing to the police.

"I feel like maybe the murder board situation from Monday might bely that assertion just a bit, but I am glad to hear you aren't nosing around too much," Tuck said as he studied my face. "You okay?"

I sighed. "Yeah, angry enough to spit, but okay." I looked over his shoulder at Jared. "Thanks for preparing me back there." I smiled widely.

He blushed and nodded. "Just wanted you to see what there was to see with our assurance behind you." He smiled warmly and then glanced at Tuck. "Nothing amiss in here, I hope," he said in a more official voice.

I took the hint and shook my head. "Nothing. I walked the whole floor, and everything looks fine." I took a look around the store again, but I still didn't see anything out of sorts.

"Good, but it does concern me," Tuck said, "that someone went to the trouble of vandalizing your store in such an intentional way."

I tilted my head and looked at him. "Isn't all vandalism intentional?"

He nodded. "Yes, but this required them to get a ladder, and they didn't just scrawl across the windows. They damaged the name of your store. That feels quite deliberate, not just angry."

I hadn't thought about it that way, and the idea of someone taking that much time and effort to say something hateful to me made me need to sit down. I moved hazily toward the register and leaned against the stool. "When you put it that way . . ." I braced myself with both hands against the stool. "But what does someone think I'm being hypocritical about?"

Jared shook his head. "We were hoping you could tell us. Has anyone said anything like that to you recently?"

"No, nothing like that." I wracked my brain trying to figure out why someone would think I was a hypocrite. I tried really hard to be the same person publicly that I was privately. I looked at Tuck, "Could this have to do with the murder?"

Tuck shrugged. "I really don't know, Harvey. It could be about anything, a book you've recommended, your recycling event, the murder, your romantic life." He winked at me as he said that one, and I worked hard to keep from letting my eyes flash over to meet Jared's. "I expect someone saw something about the crime that they just didn't recognize as important, so we'll ask around."

"But in the meantime, why don't you call me before you walk home? I'll give you a police escort," Jared added.

Tuck chuckled. "I bet you will," he said under his breath as he headed over into the café, where Rocky was starting her first pot of the day.

"Well, I won't decline that offer," I said with a smile. "But not because I think I need the escort."

Jared blushed. "I guess our secret's out," he said.

"Oh, I think we can safely say that as soon as someone saw me walking near your house the rumor mill started, even without Margie to staff it." I smiled and squeezed his arm. "I get off at five tonight."

"I'll be here," he said and then turned to join Tuck, who had two large coffees, at the front door. Both men waved as they headed out, and I took a deep breath as I noticed Woody already on a ladder taking down the sign.

When I stepped outside to thank him, he was just passing the heavy piece of wood down to Marcus, who stared at the graffiti with a deep frown. "Who would do this, Harvey?"

I shook my head. "I have no idea, but whoever it is clearly has something they want to have heard." I turned to Woody. "Jared said you think you can fix this."

Woody sighed. "I don't know about that, Harvey. Spray paint sinks pretty deep into the wood grain. I can reuse the wood for something else after I plane it down, but I worked up a little something last night. I was hoping to give it to you when you opened the new addition, but now is as good a time as any.

He walked over to his truck, lifted a tarp, and pulled out a new sign that said All Booked Up in letters that were cut into the wood with a router and then painted gold against the deep burgundy red backdrop of the painted wood behind them.

I gasped. "Woody, this is gorgeous. You made this last night? How? Why?"

A wave of color washed up Woody's neck. "I liked the wood-burned look when you were just starting out. It felt rustic, spunky." He laughed. "But now that you run an established business, I wanted you to have something more fitting, more polished."

Marcus ran his hands over the front. "You did this in one night?"

Woody laughed. "It's just a router on a template. Totally easy. And the painting was therapeutic. I even turned on some Bob Ross for inspiration."

"I love that," I said but then pretended to frown. "I don't see any happy little trees though."

"Turn it over," Woody said with a sly grin.

When Marcus flipped over the wood, there in the corner was Woody's signature, burned into the wood, and one little snow-covered pine tree next to it. I grinned and hugged my friend whose humor had just improved the morning exponentially. "Let's get this thing up there," I said.

Woody smiled and ascended the ladder before Marcus handed him the sign, and the woodworker screwed it into the two-by-four pieces he'd attached to the brick for the previous sign.

I stepped back off the curb, after being sure nothing was coming, and examined my new sign. It looked perfect, just red enough to stand out from the brick but also coordinated perfectly. Woody really had an eye for color, even if he claimed all he understood was wood.

"That looks amazing," Mart said as she joined me at the edge of the road. "What brought on the new sign?"

I sighed. "Vandalism."

She gave me a little side eye and said, "I need caffeine for this story."

"Agreed." As the two men finished hanging the side and storing the ladder in the back of the store where it lived, I flipped on the neon OPEN sign and then headed to the café with Mart, where we each got the largest vanilla latte that Rocky had available.

With our soup-bowl-size mugs in hand, we headed back to the register in the bookstore, where we could chat while I helped customers. Thursdays were, for whatever reason, a little slow in the store, and this morning was no exception. I took heart, though, that slow Thursdays usually meant booming weekends, as if everybody saved up their book money on Thursday to spend Friday through Sunday. I didn't fault that strategy at all.

Once I'd caught Mart up on the events of the morning, she sipped her drink and said, "I know this isn't going to be pleasant to hear, Harvey, but do you think someone is accusing you of being a gossip like Margie?"

Tears flew to my eyes, and I stared at my best friend hoping she hadn't meant to imply what she just implied.

"Oh no, Harvey. I don't mean that you are a gossip." She dropped her head into her hand. "Sorry, that came out wrong. I was thinking about our gathering here on Monday, about the murder board and the way we had it facing toward the window for those few minutes."

I kept staring at Mart, trying to forget the momentary hurt and concentrate on what she said. The look on her face, one of concern and regret, won me over, and I forced my thoughts back to Monday. I had set the white board up facing the front windows until Marcus had spun it around for me. "I guess someone might have seen it."

"Not just someone, Harvey. What if the killer saw it? Saw their name on the board?" Her face was stern.

I felt the blood rush out of my hands. "They would think I was just like Margie, gossiping about other people in town." I sat down hard on the stool behind me. "I can't seem to stay out of trouble, Mart."

She put her forehead against mine. "You did nothing wrong, Harvey. You wanted to help your dad and Symeon, and nothing you put on that board was untrue or secret. Everything you posted was public knowledge."

I swallowed. "Not everything." Pickle's client's name wasn't up there, but if she saw the board and thought . . ." We have to tell him."

"Already know," Pickle said as he strolled across the shop. "She and I talked the next morning. She never said anything at all about being in town that night, and I don't think she vandalized your store, Harvey."

I stared at him. "You're sure?"

"Well, I can't be sure, but I expect that if Tuck asks around, he won't hear that a person matching my client's description was seen on a ladder at your shop last night." Pickle squeezed my arm. "I'm sorry about this, though."

"Thanks," I said. "Any chance your client killed Margie Riordan?" I asked knowing full well that my friend would not answer that question.

In true and ethical form, he just stared at me and then changed the subject. "I hear an expansion is in the works."

I smiled. "Yes, starting, ceremonially, on Saturday."

"Ceremonially? From what I hear, sledgehammers will be involved." Pickle laughed. "That's a loud sort of ceremony."

"What are you talking about? Who told you that?" I asked as I looked from Mart to Pickle.

"Your daddy, woman. He just updated his will with me this morning and mentioned they were starting work on Saturday." Pickle frowned. "Not what you planned."

"Well, we are having a big recycling event in the parking lot that day. Not sure we can get construction equipment and lots of people in the same space," Mart answered.

"Sounds like Dad and I need to talk," I sighed. "Good to see you, Pickle. Catch you at home later, Mart?"

"Yes. Let's see what happens with Elijah and Hayley. Maybe with some peanut butter popcorn?" She said with a smile. "We deserve it."

"We totally deserve it," I said and then hugged her and patted Pickle on the back before slipping into the back room to call Dad.

It was a good thing I did, too, because Dad was, indeed, going to bring in a bulldozer and a dumpster on Saturday. "Mom didn't tell you?" I asked after I explained the scope of our event on Saturday.

"She said she was helping you with a recycling thing. I thought it would involve a few extra trashcans." Dad sighed. "We can hold off until Sunday. No problem. Do you think we can park the equipment at the back of the lot, though. The rentals all start on Saturday, and I'd like to have everything delivered as scheduled just to avoid confusion and more cost."

"Sure, Dad. As long as we have the front half to gather materials, we should be fine." I hoped I was right. When Mom was involved, things I planned tended to double in size.

"Sounds good, honey. Sorry for the mix-up," he said. "I'm just a little eager to get started."

"I love that, Daddy," I said. "And I'm glad everything went well with the closing yesterday. Levine didn't give you any trouble?"

"Not a bit. In fact, he was really subdued." He paused. "It

was odd, really. Didn't seem himself, but I didn't question it. I'll take my wins where I can get them."

"Me, too," I said and ended the call.

A subdued Edgar Levine . . . now that was something I wanted to see. I wondered for a split second if the real estate mogul might have climbed a ladder to destroy my sign. But then I decided that, if anything, he would have ordered one of his lackeys to do it.

The idea totally slipped my mind, though, when a tiny girl walked up to me and said, "Could you help me find the Doc McStuffins books?" I smiled at her and then looked up to see a man with her same eyes smiling at his daughter.

"Absolutely," I said and began to walk toward the children's section. The tiny girl took my hand, and I felt warmth spread up my arm. "So which ones do you have?"

"The whale one, the knight one, the bubble one . . ." she continued to list most of the titles that I recognized from the Doc McStuffins's library.

I looked over my shoulder at her dad, and he grinned. "She's looking for the one about Boomer the soccer ball and the one about the owl." His voice was full of pride.

"Ah, then let me show you our whole Doc section, okay? I think we have those two on hand, and if not, I can order them and have them here by Monday," I said.

"Oh, I hope you have them. I can hardly wait," the little girl said as she bounced up and down so hard that the collection of tiny braids on her head moved in time.

I pointed father and daughter to the shelf, and they both knelt down and began to flip through. I was only a few steps away when I heard the first squeal of delight, and the second followed soon after. I was glad we had both titles she wanted, and I made a note to be sure that we ordered the full collection in case she found any more titles she needed to fill out her own shelves.

The rest of the afternoon went by in a similar fashion, and by the time five o'clock rolled around, I had almost forgotten – almost – that Jared was meeting me to walk me home. But when he came in with a low-slung baseball hat, jeans, and a flannel shirt on, I sucked in my breath. Casual was an even better look on him than his uniform.

"You ready?" he asked as he made his way to the register, where I was just gathering my things.

"I am," I said as I caught a whiff of something evergreen scented. "You smell amazing."

"Thanks," he said as he took my hand and leaned over to kiss my cheek.

Marcus gave me a wink as we headed out the door, and I couldn't help but grin back.

I let Jared take the dogs' leashes when he offered and enjoyed watching as he got his balance against the combined force of two hounds bent on a good sniff. He mastered their wily ways quickly, though, and soon we were strolling down the street as if this was a simple pastime, not something designed to keep me safe from deranged vandals.

"We got a report of someone on a ladder by your store last night," he said. "Although, it wasn't a particularly helpful description since the witness said they thought it was you."

"Me? Why would I vandalize my own sign," I said as I stopped dead in the middle of the sidewalk.

Jared turned toward me. "You wouldn't, but the witness didn't think anything of you being on a ladder in front of your own store. So he didn't pay much attention to what you were doing up there."

"But it wasn't me." I said with a whimper.

Jared pulled me back into our stroll. "We know. But it sounds like someone wanted it to look like you."

"What did the witness say?"

"Gorgeous woman, about five-five with curly brown hair and blue shoes." He shrugged.

"The witness said 'gorgeous?'" I quirked an eyebrow in his direction.

"Okay, maybe I'm embellishing, but the height, hair, and shoes were verbatim." He squeezed my hand.

I sighed. "Well, I don't own blue shoes, but I could see how someone might think I could." I looked down at my bright red Born Mary Janes and laughed.

"Would you ever want blue shoes?" Jared asked with a smile.

"Maybe. Royal blue Doc Martens would be cool," I said. "I've always wanted a pair of Docs but couldn't afford them when they were trendy and age-appropriate."

A smile turned up one corner of Jared's mouth. "For what it's worth, I think you'd look amazing in blue Docs," he said. "As long as you didn't use them to kick my tail."

"Well, don't do anything worth getting a tail-kicking, and you won't have to worry," I said.

We had reached my house, and I found I really didn't want to go inside. But knowing that we had a date the next night helped me let go of his hand, at least long enough to give him a kiss before walking to my door. "Thank you for the escort, Officer," I said.

"Anytime, ma'am. Anytime." He smiled and turned to walk away as I walked the last few feet onto our stoop. Then, I screamed.

There, in a pile on my stoop, were a bunch of doll heads all with their mouths taped shut.

8

J ared was by my side in seconds, and Mart flung open the door at about the same moment. All three of us and the dogs stood staring at the creepy display on the concrete, and then Jared took out his phone and called Tuck.

Thank goodness for leashes because Taco lunged toward the stack and almost grabbed what looked to be the severed head of a Cabbage Patch Doll to use as a chew toy. Mart stepped over the pile and took the leashes to lead the dogs into the backyard away from temptation. If the gift hadn't been so very creepy, the hound's reaction might have been funny, even desirable.

But as Jared confirmed when he finished his call, we needed to not disturb anything. "There might be fingerprints," he said as he put his arm around my waist and pulled me toward him.

"Right. I've seen that on *Criminal Minds*. The unsub leaves fingerprints on the tape residue," I was only half-joking, but it was good to see a smile on Jared's face.

"Precisely Agent Beckett. Precisely." He motioned toward the garden bench Mart had given me for my last birthday so I could watch the finches in the patch of sunflowers I planted. "Let's sit."

I nodded and let him lead me over. I dropped onto the seat and felt the tears begin. I wasn't sobbing, just overwhelmed that someone would violate my house this way, especially after my store had been vandalized. It was awful and terrifying. "Why would someone have done this?" I asked, mostly to myself.

"This is definitely a threat, Harvey. Someone wants you – or I guess it could be Mart," he looked toward the fenced backyard where she was throwing a tennis ball for the dogs to watch fly across the yard and then leave there, "but given the vandalism at the store, I think we can safely assume someone is sending a message."

I nodded. "Yeah," I said as I sank against the seat back. "But why?"

Jared shook his head and leaned back next to me as he stared up at the sky. "Have you said anything about the case to anyone?"

"No. After Monday night when we all brainstormed suspects, not a word. I've been so caught up in the plans to expand the store and now the fundraiser that I haven't really had any time to think much about the murder." When I put it like that, I felt a little guilty. Margie deserved better than that, much as I disliked her. Still it was true.

Jared sighed. "We'll figure it out, Harvey." Silenced settled like a gentle shawl over our shoulders for a few moments.

But then, tires squealing behind us jarred both us to our feet. Symeon was already out of the car and racing toward the house.

"Stop," Jared yelled in a voice of authority that I had never heard but would definitely heed, and Symeon pitched forward as his feet slipped to a stop.

"It's at the front door, Sy," I said. "It's a crime scene. Mart is out back."

Symeon's shoulders rose and fell, and then he took a couple of steps back before walking our way. Mart came through the back gate and joined us by the sunflowers. "Sorry. I got your text," Sy said to Mart. "I wasn't thinking."

Mart hugged him. "We're both okay. It's good to see you, though."

I sighed and looked at the two of them and then over at Jared, who was watching me. "We are okay, but we have to figure this out."

Tuck arrived at that moment, and Jared squeezed my hand before going to meet his boss.

"I'm glad he was with you when you found it," Mart said to me.

"Me, too. I might have kicked the whole thing across the yard if he hadn't been. So creepy." I shivered a bit to shake off the bad vibe. Then, I looked as the ashen pallor to Symeon's skin. "Sy, sit down. You look like you're going to pass out."

Mart glanced over and then tugged him toward the bench. "Are you okay?" she asked.

He took a deep breath and nodded. "It's just been a day." He pulled Mart down beside him and pulled her close. "Someone left a pile of rotting mussels outside Max's back door today. They spelled out the words 'Stop talking' in putrid seafood."

Just the thought of it made me gag, and I turned away from my friends to get myself together. When I opened my eyes, Jared and Tuck were walking my way. Tuck's face was drawn.

"This is the fourth incident today," he said as he approached.

"Fourth?" Symeon asked as he stood. "What was the other one?"

"Someone left Elle a warning in deadheaded flowers at her greenhouse this afternoon," Tuck said.

Mart barked out a laugh. "A flower petal warning? Was that supposed to be scary?" She stopped talking, though, when she saw the look on Tuck's face.

"It said, "Shut up" and someone dug what looked like a grave in one of her flower beds." Tuck's face was anything but comical. "Even gave me the willies."

All the hair stood up on my arms, and I hugged myself. Jared stepped over and put his arm around me again. "Someone is sending a very clear message," he said as he rubbed my shoulder and tugged me close.

Tuck's phone pinged, and he pulled it out the holster on his belt. He read the screen and said, "I need to get back downtown. Cate and Lucas have similar scenes at the co-op and the museum." His phone sounded again. "And now Bear has one by his car."

Mart groaned. "That only leaves Stephen, and Walter. If he knew where you lived, Harvey..."

I was already dialing. Stephen answered on the first ring. "Harvey, we just found something. I was about to call Tuck."

"He's with me. We've all gotten them."

"Gotten what?" Stephen asked.

"Messages telling us to keep quiet." I looked at my friends and then said, "Can we come over?"

"I'll put the kettle on and some bourbon out." He hung up the phone, and we all headed for our cars. It was time to talk this through.

WITHIN MINUTES, Jared, Mart, Symeon, and I were on the road to where Bear's car was parked at the hospital before we went on our way to Stephen and Walter's, the dogs stowed in the house with dinner and new chew toys. Tuck was meeting Cate and Lucas at the museum and then going to see what was left at the co-op. Jared's knee was bouncing, so I put my hand over his where he sat next to me in the passenger's seat.

"Yeah, just wish we had more officers at a time like this," he said as he glanced at his phone. "Every minute later . . ."

I squeezed his fingers. "You are going to figure this out, and we are going to help."

Mart leaned forward and put her hand on Jared's shoulder. "Consider us your bonus deputies."

A furrow formed between Jared's eyebrows.

"Deputies who talk things through, take no action, and report everything to you," I said with a small smile.

He glanced over at me, and I saw the corners of his eyes crease. *That's better*, I thought as we pulled into the hospital lot. Bear was by his car, and there in syringes were the words "Stop Talking." Clearly this person had a flare for the terrifying.

Jared took some pictures, spoke with Bear for a few minutes, and then got back into Symeon's car. "Bear and Henri will be meet us there," he said as he put the phone to his ear to speak to Tuck and report what he'd found.

A few minutes later, Symeon pulled into our friends' drive-way. I felt a little nervous that this was the first time most of my friends were going to find out that Jared and I were dating, if that's what having one date with plans for a second was called, but it couldn't be helped. We had bigger problems.

Walter came right down and led Jared around the back of the house while Mart, Symeon, and I climbed the steps to their front door. My phone rang just was we headed in, so I hung back and answered the call from my mom, afraid to hear what she'd say.

"Harvey, are you okay?" Mom said.

I paused, took a breath, and said, "Of course, why?"

I heard her exhale. "Someone left a note on our door, and it scared me. I thought maybe—"

"Come to Stephen and Walter's, but don't move the note

and take some pictures. And let Tuck know," I said without letting her finish.

Normally, my mother couldn't stop asking questions until she understood everything about everything, but this time, she must have heard something in my voice because she said, "Alright. See you in ten minutes."

When I stepped inside the house, the mood was somber. Rocky and Marcus were sitting quietly with a magazine on the couch. Bear was leaning on the counter, two fingers of bourbon in a cut glass in his hand with Henri rubbing his back. Elle was nearby, her own dark liquid in hand. She looked shaken. I gave her a hug and then turned to Bear and Henri and asked, "You okay?"

He nodded and took a long pull from his drink.

I groaned and sank onto the couch. "So we all got some form of the same message."

"Seems like it," Stephen said as he handed me my own glass of liquor. "Ours said, "Be quiet" in driftwood on the riverside.'"

Mart, never one to think a moment too heavy for a joke, said, "That was a risky endeavor. The tide is coming in. They could have missed their entire point of intimidation with one rogue wave." She smiled.

Stephen winked. "We thought of that, too, but sadly, they did not." He took a sip from his glass. "This is about Margie's murder, I suppose."

I shook my head. "I guess. I really have no idea. Have any of you been talking about the murder with anyone?"

Everyone shook their heads.

"No, not really," Symeon said. "Max and I have chatted about it a little, but casually. It just seemed pretty likely that Edgar Levine was the guy, right?"

Henri nodded. "That's what I thought. Cate and I talked about it a bit, but we didn't even mention names, didn't say anything about who might have done it. Just talked about how sad it was that Margie had died."

Stephen looked at her. "Sad? The woman was a busybody. I mean she didn't deserve to die, but . . ."

"Right," Henri snapped. "She didn't deserve to die." She gave Stephen a pointed look and then turned to look over the water. "Just think how lonely she must have been to be that interested in everyone else's life. That's the real tragedy."

I swallowed. "I hadn't thought of it that way."

"Me neither," Rocky said.

A heavy silence floated over us all, and I let myself disappear into the sound of the waves outside for a few minutes.

Then, a knock sounded at the front door, and Mom and Dad came in followed closely by Cate and Lucas. "Tuck went to the condo," Mom said, "but Lu is coming over with tacos."

I stood up and hugged my mom. "Of course you would think of food. Thanks."

"Actually, it was Lu who thought of it when Tuck called her to let her know he'd be late." Lu was Tuck's wife, and she ran the best food truck around. Her Mexican dishes, especially her mole, were notorious for being the best comfort food in a hundred miles.

"I'll get the table set up." Stephen headed into the kitchen with Mart close behind, and they began to set the long farm table by the wall of windows overlooking the ocean.

I sat back down next to Symeon. "You aren't working tonight?"

He shook his head. "I told Max I needed the night off after we found our message." He shuddered. "I helped him clean up, and then he sent me home to rest."

I nodded. "Glad you can be here," I said. "You okay?"

"I think so. Tuck hasn't asked to talk me again, so maybe I'm not really a suspect anymore."

Dad sat down in a chair across from us, a glass of bourbon

in hand. "I imagine that the fact that we received these threats too may get us both off the hook as suspects."

Symeon gave Dad a small smile. "I certainly hope so." He looked down at his hands and then up at Dad again. "So how did you get your message?"

"A note scrawled on a twenty-dollar bill. You?"

"Rotting seafood," Symeon said, and then the two men began to laugh. I took that as my cue that they were both fine and went to find Mom.

She, Henri, and Cate were standing against the railing of Stephen and Walter's deck looking out over the river beyond. It was a breezy evening, which was a gift since it helped lift the humidity and also pushed the mosquitoes into someone else's space. But even with the lovely night, the mood was heavy.

I stood silently at the railing, sipping my drink and watching the waves. I didn't know what to say.

Finally, Cate broke the silence. "Clearly someone is targeting our friend group, right?"

"Sure looks like," Cate added, "but why?"

I took another sip of my drink as I thought back to Monday, the only time when all of us had been together. I let my mind move over the faces there, and as I called up where everyone was sitting that night, I ticked off the way each of them had been threatened. As best I could remember, everyone in that room had gotten a message, so it seemed almost irrefutable that this was about that gathering.

Mom stirred and said, "Has anyone checked in with Woody? I wonder if he's gotten some kind of threat."

I stood bolt upright. "Woody wasn't there," I whispered.

"What?" Cate said turning toward me.

"Woody wasn't there on Monday night. He said he had somewhere else to be. I just remembered." I pulled my phone out of my back pocket and called him. He answered on the second ring. "Woody, anything weird happen today?"

He paused a second and said, "Aside from a piliated wood-pecker flying into my living room and trying to dissect my bookshelf?"

I chuckled. "Well that is weird, but yeah, aside from that." I could feel Mom, Cate, and Henri staring, but I kept my eyes on the water so I couldn't get distracted.

"Nope, nothing." His voice grew heavier. "Why? What happened?"

"Are you free to come to Stephen and Walter's?" I asked.

"Be there in five." He hung up.

"Woody didn't get a message," I said. "Because he wasn't there on Monday."

"Hot dog," Henri said with a shout. "You figured it out, Harvey Beckett?" Her face grew somber. "But that means someone saw something that made them target us."

I sighed. "Yeah."

Tuck, Walter, and Jared walked up the decks from the river-bank. "Seems that way," Tuck agreed. "I need to know more about exactly what happened on Monday."

The six of us joined the others inside, and after Stephen refilled our glasses – iced tea for Jared and Tuck; more bourbon for the rest of us – Tuck asked us to walk him through Monday night at the store.

But before we could get started, Lu arrived with two trays of hot tacos and another of churros. When the scent reached me, I realized I was starving and put myself first in line to eat. No one ever said I was shy about food.

The line snaked around Stephen and Walter's kitchen island, and one by one we each sat down to eat Lu's delicious contribution. Between bites, we all said our thank yous. Tuck had already caught her up on the day's events, but she had missed the revelation about Woody. I filled her in before getting up for another churro.

When Tuck repeated his request that we tell him about our

time together on Monday, Mom started explaining the events of the evening, adding details as Tuck asked about things like when everyone arrived, where we sat, and what we specifically talked about. When Mom mentioned the white board, Mart and I looked at each other.

Mart interrupted Mom before she continued her narrative. "Harvey accidentally set the board up facing the street at first."

Tuck sat up straighter. "So someone walking by could have seen what you were writing?"

I nodded. "Yeah," Jared scooted his bar stool closer to me and took my hand. "It's my fault," I whispered.

Cate stood and marched over to me. "Seriously, Harvey, I have to give *you* this lecture now? It's not your fault that any of this is happening. The person responsible for these threats is the person who made them, not you."

I smiled. This was Cate's solid refrain, especially to women because we so often took the blame for things that were not our responsibility. And she was right. I knew she was right, but I still felt guilty.

"This isn't on you at all, Harvey," Jared added. "Someone is nervous about how much you all know."

Just then, a knock sounded at the door, and Woody came in. "Clearly, I'm missing some party," he said.

"Sadly, not a fun one," Lucas said. "But I'm glad you aren't a part of this particular club."

Tuck took a moment to explain to Woody what had happened to the rest of us that day and then said, "But you weren't there Monday when they were discussing Margie's murder, so we think that's why you didn't get a threat."

"Lucky me," he said. "Monday, oh yeah, I was at our Lion's Club meeting. We were planning our back-to-school drive."

I smiled. I hadn't even known Woody was part of the Lion's Club, but it made perfect sense that he would be. He was one of the most generous people I know, and that was saying something.

"That's right. I had forgotten about that," Bear said.

A prickle ran over my spine. "Where is Pickle tonight?"

Bear and Henri looked at each other. "We checked with him. He didn't get a threat either."

"But he was with us Monday," Symeon said.

Another moment passed between Henri and Bear. "He was," Bear said.

"And one of the people on your murder board was his client?" Jared said with a long look at Tuck.

"She was," Mart said quietly.

"I think we best go talk to Pickle," Tuck said as he and Jared both stood. "As they say, he's got some 'splaining to do."

I rolled my eyes at Tuck's terrible Lucille Ball impression, but my heart sank. Pickle was about to be in, well, quite the pickle.

Before he left, Jared leaned over and gave me a gentle kiss. "Call you later?"

I smiled, but as soon as he and Tuck left, everyone seemed to lean toward me. Only Cate spoke, though. "So you and Officer Watson, huh?"

I blushed so hard I felt my hair stand up. "It's kind of new."

"Looks kind of hot, too," Henri said, and then all the men in the room stood up and went onto the deck without saying a word. And they made fun of women when we went to the bathroom together.

"So dish?" Cate said.

I glanced over at my mom, who was grinning ear to ear. The woman was past the point of pressuring me about grandchildren, thank goodness, but she still wanted to see me happy. And to her, a partner meant happiness . . . and with Dad as her partner, I couldn't blame her for thinking that way, even if I didn't always share her perspective.

Once I stopped blushing and finished my drink, I told my friends and mother about my date with Jared, about our plans for the next night, and a bit about how excited I was.

They, of course, were over the moon and curious about details, which I didn't give, but I did tell them that I really liked him. "He's really special," I said, and everyone got all mushy.

So before we got too sentimental from romance and alcohol, I stood up and said I was ready to go home. Mart, knowing how much I hated too much attention on my romantic relationships, joined me on my stroll to the door and waved for Symeon to join us, and soon, the other women were gathering their men as we all said goodbye to Walter and Stephen.

On the ride home, the three of us sat in silence until I needed to know where to take Symeon. He occasionally slept over on our couch, and I didn't mind that at all. But tonight, he said he should go home so he could get to the restaurant early the next morning. Mart gave me directions to his cute boathouse on the bay side of town, and while I scrolled through my phone as distraction, they said their goodnight.

After Mart got back in the car, I said, "You two seem really happy."

It was her turn to blush, I could see out of the corner of my eye, as she said, "We are. I think, well, I think maybe he's the one I'm going to pick."

"You mean forever?" I said, trying to sound casual even as I wanted to squeal.

"Yeah," she said quietly. "Yeah, forever."

I let the quiet fill up the car again as we drove because, well, it was a nice thing for my best friend to have someone she loved . . . and it was even nicer to think I might have found my someone, too.

9

The next morning, I definitely felt the effects of two glasses of bourbon, but two big glasses of water and some coffee got me moving for the opening shift at the store. Given that the dogs had been tucked away at the house all evening with no company, they were eager to meet and greet on our walk in. Their motivations and mine were unfortunately mismatched since all I wanted to do was avoid everyone, but the pups were persistent. So I slapped on my best "good to see you but don't talk to me grin" that I usually reserved for plane rides and let them greet everyone.

By the time we reached the store, all three of us were tired, but unlike the dogs, I couldn't just go curl up on a soft pillow and sleep the day away. We only had one more day until the recycling event, and I needed to be sure we were spreading the word. Mom was coming by this morning to help me check that we had all the supplies ready, thank goodness. I definitely needed her help.

Plus, Dad, Walter, and Woody were on their way over to get their construction plans for Sunday all laid out. Between their presence, the need to plan this big event, and the usual Friday rush, it was going to be all I could do to make it through the day. Fortunately, I had my date with Jared to look forward to, and since Mart had already left town, I was hoping to cut out early, clean up the house, and get most of the meal ready to cook before he came.

Then, I had this little fantasy of us cooking together for a bit before enjoying a quiet night in the backyard. In fact, I was so deep in my imagining as I checked the supplies at the front counter that I was a little surprised when I looked up at the sound of a knock and saw Jared smiling at me.

As I walked over to let him in, I tried to temper my smile, but when I saw how happy he looked as he leaned over and kissed my cheek, I decided that playing it cool wasn't necessary here and let my giddiness shine through. "It's so good to see you," I said as I reached up to hug him.

"Now, that's my kind of greeting," he said before sighing. "I only wish seeing you was the only reason I was here."

I echoed his sigh. "Me, too, but our personal lives aren't the only things we have going on. You've got news about," I looked around as if someone might hear in the still empty store, "what we discussed last night."

"I do," he said. "Have a minute?" He took my hand and kissed it, and for a second, I felt the burden of all that had happened lift.

"Sure. Chocolate milk okay?" I said as I led him toward the café. "I'm not sure I'm up for brewing coffee just yet."

"Chocolate milk is more than okay," he said as he picked a table back from the windows and sat down. "Thanks."

I grabbed two boxes of the chocolate milk that Rocky kept for children and returned to the table with Jared. When I sat down, he grinned, slipped the straw into the top of the box, and drained it in one pull. "Just like being back in elementary school, but without the smell of tater tots."

I shivered and laughed. "Oh my. Tater tots. That's a food that shouldn't exist."

"Are you kidding me? Have you ever had them baked with some really good cheddar and a little chives? So delicious," he said as he put his fingers to his lips and kissed them.

"You'll have to prove that." I grinned across the table at him.

"Is that a challenge, ma'am?" he twanged in a far deeper Southern accent than his normal.

"Only if you're up for it." I winked at him and sat back, eager to continue the banter but also so very curious and nervous about his conversation with Pickle. "Are you sure it's okay that you tell me this?" I asked.

Jared nodded. "Both Pickle and Tuck agreed that it was good to keep you all in the loop, at least in a minimal way, since you were all victims. But everyone has to be very cautious to not talk about anything related to this case when others can hear. Understood?" He had slipped into his professional voice, and I was finding even that voice very appealing.

"Pickle cannot tell us who his client is. That's a brief of his position as her lawyer, but he did tell us that he did not receive any threats yesterday, that he had spoken with his client about the threats you all received, and that she assured him she was not responsible," Jared said as he reached across the table and took my hand.

I shook my head. "But that's not any real information. How does that help?" The frustration was rising in my throat.

"It confirms that it was, probably, his client after all, despite what he was obliged to tell us as her attorney. If he did not get a threat but was here on Monday . . ." He rubbed a small circle on the skin between my thumb and fingers.

I took a deep breath. "Okay, but we still don't know who she is?"

Jared shook his head. "That we will have to figure out through good old police work." He pulled my hand closer to him. "We will figure it out, Harvey, but for now, everyone needs to stay alert, pay attention to anything strange, and also be sure to not move around alone."

I groaned. "I'm so tired of having to be escorted everywhere." Over and over again, I kept ending up in situations where I couldn't be alone, and as an introvert, I needed alone time. I sighed heavily and then met Jared's gaze.

He was waggling his eyebrows. "Well, if it helps, I don't mind being your escort as often as you need me." He half-stood, leaned over the table, and kissed me. "In fact, that's my assigned duty for the time being – escort to Harvey's coterie."

I laughed. "You make me sound like some sort of princess."

"If the glass shoe fits," he said and pulled me to my feet. "Now, what can I do to help you this morning?"

I smiled and headed toward the register. "Mind dusting?" I said as I held up the small bin of single socks Mart and I collected for this purpose.

"That depends. Do I get to take all the books off the shelves and do it for real?" He took two socks and the bottle of wood treatment from my hands.

"Knock yourself out, slugger. I don't usually go that hard-core, but I'm sure the store could use it." I leaned over and kissed his cheek. "Thanks. I'm going to let everyone else know, by text, what you just told me, if that's okay."

"Good plan, and stress the part about not being alone, okay? For everyone. We don't need any macho man thinking he's beyond needing company," Jared said as he turned toward the front of the store.

After adding Jared to our group text, I sent a note with all the information Jared had provided as well as his caution about being alone and a reminder that we had to be really careful about what we talked about where. Then, I put my phone on the counter so that I wasn't distracted by the rush of replies that I was sure would come and took my own dust rag and polish to begin on the front tables. If we were going to do this, we might as well do it right.

BY THE TIME Marcus and Rocky arrived an hour later, the store was glimmering and smelling like artificial lemon. "Ah, cleaning day," Marcus said as he tucked his skateboard behind the register.

Jared came around the last set of shelves in the reference section and handed me the polish and socks. "All done," he said.

"Thorough and efficient," I said. "Two very appealing qualities." I kissed his cheek and walked him to the door. "See you at five?" I asked as my plans of having dinner prepped early faded away.

"Definitely," he said and slipped out the door and walked toward the police station.

"I'm glad he was here," Rocky said when I walked over to get my morning coffee and pay her for the chocolate milk. "Looks like you were, too." She grinned at me.

I blushed and nodded. "I was glad to see him, and yes, for lots of reasons." I sighed as I leaned against the counter. "I just wish he'd gotten more news about Pickle's client."

Rocky sighed. "Yeah, but we also wouldn't want Pickle to do something that would jeopardize his job, right?"

She was right, and I knew it. But I couldn't help but be frustrated. Someone was threatening the people I loved, and I felt helpless. I'd learned, though, that when I felt helpless, I needed to do something that made me feel I wasn't, so I turned to Marcus and then looked at Rocky. "What do you say we kick up the music vibe in here today?"

Marcus grinned from by the register. "Backbeat playlist it is," he said as he bent over and changed the streaming station on our store stereo. U2's "Beautiful Day" started bouncing through the speakers, and I felt better already.

Right at ten when we opened, Mom and Dad both arrived with Woody and Walter close behind. They all looked a little haggard, and I couldn't blame them. I felt that way. But everyone was smiling, too, and eager to get to work.

Since I couldn't be in three places at once, I chose to do what I did best: open my store. I flipped on the OPEN sign, unlocked the door, and smiled. A small group was waiting to come in, and I greeted each person, old friend and new, as they came through the door.

The blonde woman with the braid who had wanted an edgier novel to read was back, and I grinned as she stepped in. "You're back?" I said.

She smiled back. "I am. I'm on leave from work and reading fast. Got anymore recommendations for me?"

"Absolutely. Let's go," I said as we walked back toward the fiction section. "I thought of this as soon as you left last time, and you've probably read it." I pulled *Lolita* from the shelf. "But if you can handle the, um, unusual nature of Humbert Humbert's love, the language is beautiful."

"I have read it, but you know, it's been a long time. I'll give it a go again. Thanks," she took the paperback from my hands. "What else?

"Since we're doing classics, have you read *Clockwork Orange*?" I said.

"I didn't even know there was a book, but I loved the movie. Great," she said. "Now one more?"

"Oh, that makes me think of another book-to-film adaptation. Have you read *Winter's Bone*?" I pulled the slim title from the shelf.

"No, and I haven't seen that film either. Looks like I know what I'll be doing this afternoon. Thanks, Harvey," she said as she moved toward Marcus at the register.

I smiled and turned back to the shelves, taking note of where we had room and what I might order to fill in the gaps. It had been a good week, and the weekend was only going to be better. So I took out my phone and began to make a list.

I got distracted, though, when I heard our customer ask Marcus about the murder at the post office. When I looked up, Marcus was nodding and shooting glances at me but not saying anything. I sighed and walked over just in time to hear the customer say, "I heard that postmistress woman was really nosy."

"We've heard the same thing, but since she's dead . . ." I said casually but clearly. "Anything else we can help you with today?"

The woman looked from me to Marcus. "No, I guess not. Thanks." She held up her three books and headed into the cafe.

"That was weird," Marcus said with a shake of his head. "Or maybe I'm just a little paranoid what with everything."

I sighed. "I thought it was weird, too, but yeah, who knows? I'm going to let Jared know, though, just in case."

Marcus nodded. "Sounds good. And your mom asked me to tell you that she could use a minute if you have one."

I glanced over to where Mom was working in the front window of the café. The blonde customer was sitting at the next table over, reading. It now seemed like a really good idea to talk to Mom.

As I walked over, I texted Jared to tell him about the strange conversation and let him know the woman was still here. Then, I sat down across from Mom and shifted my chair just slightly so I could see the young woman behind her. "Marcus said you wanted to see me?"

"I did. We need to talk about tomorrow," she said. "Here's the plan I have for the layout in the lot. What do you think?"

I slid the paper from in front of her and studied it. "Looks good. Just one small change." In the corner of the page, I wrote, "The woman behind you is listening in. Just be aware."

Mom pulled the paper back toward her. "Ah yes, so noted. Thanks, Harvey." She shifted in her chair. "Galen is on his way. I'm going to do an interview with him for his social, see if we can't create a little more buzz."

I smiled. "Any more buzz and we'll need to hope someone donates beehives tomorrow." I stood. "Better go see how the men are doing."

"Oh yes, I'll come with you," Mom said as she stood and folded the design plan with my note into fourths and slipped it into her purse before gathering the rest of her things. "Maybe I can lend my expertise."

"I'm sure Dad will love that," I said as I slid my arm into hers and led her out of the café. I could feel the woman's eyes on our backs, but it didn't seem like she was following us. Still, as we walked, I shot Rocky a text to ask her to give me a heads up if the woman headed back this way.

"I have an eye on the package," her reply read, and I laughed. We were all getting quite equipped for spy work, I suppose.

When Mom and I joined the men, they were all doing that thing that seems to happen when people work construction and such. Each of them had his hands on his hips, feet spread wide, and they were all staring at the shelves in the fiction section. "Are you trying to knock the wall over with the power of your minds?" I asked.

Dad turned and looked at me, "Har, Har, Har." He stepped forward and touched the shelf. "First, of all, the good news. We got our permits." He waved some pieces of paper around.

"And the bad news?" I asked.

"We can't quite figure out how to keep these books here available to customers while we build," Dad said.

Walter looked at me. "Ideally, we'd cordon off a section

here," he walked a square about eight feet into the store and about ten-feet wide, "but if we do that, you lose a whole bunch of space for your inventory."

I sighed. "Right. That makes sense. But I also don't want *all* of my inventory covered in construction dust, so I think we need to hang up that plastic sheeting stuff. I'll just have to find a place for the books. Show me what needs to go?"

Woody walked along the shelves putting green painters tape on each one that needed to move. It was about half the fiction section and the romance and mystery shelves, too. That was a lot of books.

I leaned back against our collection of Nora Roberts titles and groaned. "Okay, we'll just stack them neatly in the front window," I said, feeling disappointed that this great thing meant a few weeks of chaos in my tidy store.

"Wait," Mom said as she gazed toward the front of the store. She grabbed Walter's tape measure, measured the shelves, then walked to the display window up front. She did some measuring there and walked back. "What if we just put the shelves in the window?"

I stared at her for a minute while I tried to quell my instinctive resistance to any sort of change in my perfect bookstore. Then, I pondered a minute. "Marcus, are you free?" I called back toward the register.

"On my way," he said, and a minute later, he stood nodding along as Mom shared her plan. "I think that sounds really doable."

"Maybe we can make a sign that says, 'Pardon our dust.'" I suggested.

"Or what about, 'Be a fixture in the bookstore,' Marcus said. "Customers give us understanding during demolition, but they're also on display while they shop."

I smiled as Woody added, "I can build the raised dog bed

this evening so that we can add that to the window as part of the "bookstore life" theme."

I was growing to love the idea. "Let's do it," I said, and Dad clapped his hands once. "Okay, folks, we have our work cut out for us. Let's clear the front window first."

"I'll get that sign made, and make a temporary one that says "Pardon Our Dust" for the front door, too," Marcus said.

Mom loaded her arms carefully with books. "I'll start unloading the shelves and stacking them, in order," she looked at me pointedly, "near the front of the store. That way we can find them and reshelve them easily, and the men have room to move these shelves.

I stood still as everyone started to shift toward their assignments and finally said, "I guess I'll staff the bookstore," and headed toward a mother and daughter shopping in the YA section. Clearly, everyone else had the demolition process well in hand.

After helping the two women find their last summer read to share – *A Court of Thorn and Roses* by Sarah J. Maas – and confirming that the mom was okay with her daughter reading a story with some racy bits, I headed back toward the register. Rocky texted and said, "She's heading your way."

I thought about wandering the shelves to look inconspicuous but decided that since I ran the store it was probably less conspicuous if I, well, did my job. So I rang up a customer and kept my eye out for the woman's blonde braid amongst the stacks.

After a moment, I got a text from Marcus. "She's in the back of the store. She just walked into the breakroom where I'm making signs."

"What?!"

"Said she was looking for the bathroom, but I doubt it," he replied.

"Yeah." We had a huge sign, courtesy of Woody, that read

"Restrooms" hanging from the ceiling above the doors to the bathrooms, and the breakroom door sported a big old "Staff Only" sign, too. She was snooping.

I texted Jared again and asked him to come over. "She's getting nosy," I said.

"Be there in ten." Earlier, when I'd let him know she was here, he'd said to just keep an eye on her, and we had. But now, we needed back-up.

I strolled over to where the men were picking up the first bookshelf that Mom had unloaded and quietly told Dad what was going on, after making sure the woman wasn't in sight. Then, I took Mom's arm and said, a little too loudly, "Help me think about what sections we'll put in the addition?"

Mom didn't bat an eye, although that decision had already been made and was part of the design plan she had in her purse. "Sure thing."

We walked amongst the shelves, pretending to discuss the merits of having self-help further away from the main aisle for privacy or moving the small erotica section closer to the register for less privacy. All the while, both of us scanned the shelves for the young woman, who appeared to either have turned invisible or to have left without, somehow, any of us noticing.

Finally, after our last lap, Mom said, "I need to go to the bathroom." She winked at me.

"Me, too," I said, not about to let my mother check the last possible hiding place alone, and so both of us strolled into the two-stall room and surreptitiously looked under the stall doors.

I didn't see any feet, but given how every teenager in every film hides from their teacher by standing on the toilet, I didn't doubt she was hiding. So I put a finger to my lips, opened the bathroom door, walked in a progressively softer footfall, and then let it slam shut as Mom and I tucked ourselves beside the sink.

A minute later, our stealth was rewarded when the woman stepped out of the stall furthest from us, swiveled her head, saw us, and sprinted out the door. Mom gasped, but we didn't delay and both bolted after her.

Unfortunately, with her head start and apparently Olympic-ready sprinting skills, she was out of the front of the store by the time we made it past the first set of shelves. She had blazed past Marcus, who had tried to slow her down but didn't want to grab her for fear of a lawsuit, and when she whipped past Jared who was just coming up the street, he had no cause to stop her. So she got away.

Jared, however, got a good description of her, came in to confirm she was the right person, and then radioed out for Tuck and the on-loan officers that Tuck had requested from nearby Easton to keep an eye out for her. She seemed to be on foot, or at least had been smart enough to not go to her car immediately, so he was hopeful someone would see her walking.

"She had some speed, though," he said as I handed him a coffee and motioned over to the register.

"I know," Mom said. "It felt like watching a blur."

I groaned. "She was definitely hiding in here, and she was definitely snooping." I told Jared about how she'd walked right into the breakroom and then lied about looking for the bathrooms. "I just don't know what she was looking for."

Jared shook his head. "Who knows? But we'll find out when we catch her." He glanced at his watch. "Speaking of which, I've got a few more hours until," he looked at Mom, "until my plans for tonight, so I'm going to do a block-by-block search. I'll keep you posted."

He winked at me as he turned and left.

"Are you his plans?" Mom asked with a sly grin.

"None of your business," I said as I blushed and headed over to see what the men were doing.

10

T he rest of that afternoon flew by what with our need to decorate the new shelf display in the front window, the rest of the prep for the event the next day, and a really good flow of customers. I mostly helped lug books and organize the shelves once they were in the window, library-style with their short ends facing the window.

Marcus and I modified the display plan a little and added a couple of chairs and a small table in the opposite corner from the dogs' beds so that people could really sit and read in the window if they so wished. Besides, we needed to get more furniture off the floor to make room for construction, so it was a good use of space.

We also set up a couple of shelves in the café window, cookbooks and gardening books specifically, so that we could shift more of the fiction into the store itself. Then, we made clear signs for each shelf, much like a library might have, to show people what exactly they would find where and to remind ourselves about the temporary locations of everything.

Marcus created a little stencil from some leftover cardboard, so we could put a sketched hammer or measuring tape on each sign and tie them into our theme. Rocky helped us draw and used her beautiful calligraphy to finish each sign, and eventually, the store looked both like a construction zone – what with the plastic sheeting and sawhorses in the fiction section and the signage – and a whole new space that would probably frustrate some customers but hopefully also show them we were going to be providing even more for them soon. It was so exciting.

Between the addition renovation and the calls about what we were accepting tomorrow at the recycling event, my anticipation grew by the minute, and I couldn't even think about my date with Jared that evening without getting a little bounce in my step. By the time four p.m. rolled around and Marcus told me to leave early, I was fairly buzzing with excitement.

When I texted to say I was leaving a bit early, Jared said he'd be right over to walk me home and help me cook. I had been hoping he'd be okay with me walking by myself since I kind of wanted the time to pull my thoughts together, but since he insisted on escorting me, I decided to let myself be excited about the extra time with him.

Mom and Dad were both still at the store when I leashed up the dogs to head out, and I braced myself for some sort of quip about my dating life. Instead, they both hugged me, told me they'd be in at seven in the morning to help me set up, and wished me a great night. No sarcasm at all. I grinned and walked out the door to wait for Jared.

My wait was nonexistent though because my date arrived, single rose in hand, just as I hit the sidewalk. He took the dog leashes, kissed my cheek, and said, "Lead the way." I took his hand and started toward home, deciding to take the most scenic of the two scenic routes to get there.

As we walked past the cottage garden that one of my neighbors had created from every bit of grass in her front lawn, I breathed in deeply and treasured the chance to enjoy the evening with someone I liked very much. When he stopped to admire the way the landscaper had used echinacea blossoms with her black-eyed Susans, I stared at him with delight. This guy appreciated flowers and could even name them. He was definitely a keeper.

When my house was in sight, I stopped him and said, "I don't want to talk about this later tonight, but I need to know – did you find her?"

He shook his head. "We haven't, but we're still looking. Tuck will alert me if they locate her, but otherwise, shop talk is off limits." He kissed me gently. "Tonight is all about you."

I grinned as I moved us toward my house again. "Does that mean I can talk about my shop?"

He squinted at me and put on a very pensive expression. "Do you want to talk about your shop?"

I thought about the question. "Maybe just a little because I really want to tell you all about the remodeling we did today."

He smiled. "If it makes you happy, then I want to hear all about it."

I unlocked the door and held it open for him. "Perfect . . . but then, we need to have a discussion about music. Ever heard of Over The Rhine?" I asked as I pushed the door closed behind us.

The rest of the night was lovely. We cooked and made a thorough mess while we laughed, and I introduced Jared to Over The Rhine, Ellis Paul, Rhiannon Giddens, and all the other musicians I loved most. Then, somehow, he convinced me that I needed to go back in time to junior high and listen to Poison again. I still found it ridiculous music, but I enjoyed seeing him lip sync.

Three hours later, we had eaten, watched an episode of *Glow Up*, which he appreciated for its queer-positive message and extreme use of glitter, and cleaned up the kitchen from our escapades with flour for the quiche crust earlier. We ended the evening in the backyard with the dogs, a couple of hard ciders, and a beautiful array of shooting stars that seemed like maybe they had been sent just for us.

The goodnight kiss he gave me before he walked back to town was lingering and made my heart race, but when I went back inside to close down the house for the night, I was content and peaceful in a way I hadn't been in a long time, especially when he sent me a text that said, "Thank you, and sweet dreams. See you in the morning."

I went to bed smiling and slept like a log until my alarm slammed me awake at six. In my bliss the night before I had neglected to close my bedroom door, and I now had two dogs and a cat in bed with me. It was a wonderful I hadn't suffocated in the night.

As I smacked off my alarm and managed to free my legs from where they were pinned by the girth of two hound dogs, I stretched and thought about my day. Normally, Saturdays were really fun. People browsed longer and spent hours in the café, and I got to know some new neighbors and visitors to our town.

I was letting myself imagine who I might meet – a retired circus performer, a budding ballet dancer, a man who made the most incredible cherry crumble – when I suddenly remembered the recycling event. I had totally forgotten.

With the memory, though, came a surge of energy, and I jumped out of bed, took a quick and very hot shower, and skipped my morning coffee. Rocky was coming in early, too, and I knew she'd be brewing something far better than I could make from my grocery store selection. Besides, I couldn't sit still and just wanted to get this day going.

As I walked the dogs far faster than they wanted to go and hoped no one would catch me walking alone, my phone dinged with a text, and I looked down to see that Mart was also already up. "You ready for this?" her message read.

Immediately, my head filled in the heavy drumbeats of the

popular Power Supply song that I had last heard, I thought, at a college basketball game six years ago. Somehow, though, the theme felt appropriate for today, so I pulled the song up on my phone, put in my earbuds, and bounced along as I replied to Mart. "So ready."

Then I wished her well for her event that day, too, and tucked my phone back in the jeans I had opted for given how much lifting I might have to do. The music helped me pick up my pace, and when I rounded the corner to the store, I was almost jogging.

A small group was gathered out front again, and for a split second, fear crept up my neck. But then I saw it was just my parents, Walter, and Woody, and let the music overtake me again. I was still bopping along when I waved to them, unlocked the door, and went to turn on the lights.

I reluctantly removed my earbuds when my second play of the song finished and headed over to the café, where Rocky had just turned on the espresso machine. "Two shots this morning, boss?" she asked.

"I better stick with one. I could probably power the electricity in the building already. Thanks." I did a little skipping pattern on the floor.

"I can see that," Rocky said. "Maybe decaf?"

"No way. Why bother? I'll just jog everywhere if need be." I said with a smile.

Behind me, the bell over the door ran, and I looked back to see Marcus and Jared coming in. I smiled at these two great men and looked over to see Rocky was grinning, too. *Is this what love looks like?* I thought before I caught myself.

You've had two dates, Harvey. Two dates. Slow it down, I coached myself as I took my vanilla latte and left a ten-dollar bill on the counter. "For my next one, too," I said as Rocky raised an eyebrow.

"Gotcha," she said as Marcus leaned past me to give her a kiss.

I wasn't much into PDA, but at this moment, I couldn't resist and gave Jared a quick kiss on the lips before we both blushed and walked quickly outside, where Mom and Elle were beginning to set up tables. When he asked me if I walked to work alone, I said, "No, I had two bodyguards." He gave me a stern look but let the matter drop. I was grateful because I had totally failed at doing the one thing he asked of me, and I felt bad . . . but not bad enough to let that ruin my great mood.

Technically, Jared was on duty today. He and Tuck had agreed that given the fact that the Wacky Whisperer, as Mart had started calling our threat-leaver, would find anyone she wanted to target, it was wise for Jared to be on-site all day. I suspected Tuck was also doing Jared and I a kindness here at the beginning of whatever this was we were doing, and I was grateful. I liked having this man around. A lot.

When the tables for recording donations were all set at the front of the lot, Jared and I hung up the signs Mom had made to designate the areas for specific types of donations. We had building supplies in one area, furniture in another, then a huge pair of boxes to accept clothes and one for craft supplies, too. Any other miscellaneous stuff would go in one more box right near the front of the lot so that we could keep an eye on it. We didn't want to end up with a bunch of stuff we couldn't put to good use, and I knew from my own temptation to donate a lidless coffee mug that we could end up with a bunch of junk if we weren't careful.

As we hung our last sign, Jared slipped back toward where Dad, Woody, and Walter were standing because the bulldozer and dumpster were arriving. Some men, including my ex-boyfriend, would have been most interested in the heavy equipment, but Jared told me he wanted to know what Dad had paid for the dumpster since he needed one to pull down a plaster ceiling in his upstairs bathroom. I kind of liked that he was more interested in remodeling than racing, if I was honest.

I didn't have much time to think about that, though, because as I turned back to where Mom was staffing the first shift at the table, a huge, lifted pickup pulled up. Two men in cowboy hats got out and began to unload things from the truck's bed. They donated three doors, complete with frames, sixteen windows, and a bag of yarn that one of the men said he'd gotten when he thought his wife might like it but found out it was too thick for her to use for her baby blankets.

Mom thanked them profusely, handed them a coupon each for a free coffee inside, and then gave me a high five as they headed into the store. The coupons had been Rocky's idea. Wisely, she had thought we might get new customers for both her shop and mine if people had incentive to come right in after their donation. She was already right.

Once that first load arrived, it was like the donation flood gates opened. People were bringing bags and windows, couches and lamps that had, clearly in some cases, been tucked in corners of basements and barns for years if the thickness of the dust on them was an indication. Fortunately, all our friends arrived right at seven as planned, so we had plenty of help to organize and carry things.

Time flew by, and before I knew it, Symeon was setting up his new portable pizza oven in front of the store. It had been Mart's idea to invite Max, via Symeon's pizza prowess, to set up a stand for casual dining in front of the store, and I'd suggested Max put his chalk sandwich board near the pizza oven so that people knew he would be open for more formal, sit-down fare just up the street. He'd love the idea and had decided to open early to serve crepes and omelettes for the breakfast crowd.

In fact, the event had kind of energized all Main Street. Elle had put a sign on her own shop to tell people she was set up by the bookstore, and she'd brought over dozens of bouquets of flowers and several boxes of local produce to sell. The art co-op had their own donation box inside their building, and we were sending people there throughout the day to see the art even though Cate was with us and talking up the few paintings, photographs, and weavings she'd displayed around our check-in station. Even the maritime museum that Lucas managed was providing a discount to anyone who donated to the cause today.

Pizzas were baking, Lu's food truck had a line up the street, and we were accepting donations as fast as we could when Edgar Levine sauntered up the sidewalk. Fortunately, Stephen saw him coming from his position at the water cooler, where we were giving water to anyone who wanted some, donation or not, and whistled to get my attention. When I saw where he was pointing, I grabbed Jared as soon as he set down the armchair he and Pickle were carrying and gave him the heads up. He, in turn, texted Tuck, and fortunately, our long chain of information didn't get garbled in the communication telephone game.

By the time Levine wandered over to where Mom was sitting, Dad had joined her, and all of us were on high alert. "Just came by to see what you were doing with the lot you stole out from under me," Levin said to Dad in what was, I thought, supposed to sound like a joke but actually just sounded pouty and bitter.

"We're putting it to good use as you can see . . . and if you hang around for a few minutes, at eleven, we're ceremonially breaking ground for the addition to Harvey's shop." He held up a coupon. "You can grab a cup of coffee while you wait, if you'd like."

"I wouldn't set foot in that shop if my life depended on it," Levine said after looking pointedly in my direction. "The service there is terrible, and I'd rather drink coffee from a two-day-old gas station machine."

Rocky appeared on the sidewalk just as that last statement slid out of his snaky mouth, and she did the best prat fall I'd ever seen, spilling the entire contents of four, steaming cups of coffee on the man's suit pants. She even kept a straight face while doing it.

He spun on her, grabbed her by the throat, and said, "You will pay for my cleaning bill and be glad you didn't burn me." Rocky gasped against his hand.

Jared swept over, freed Rocky, and wrenched Levine's arm behind his back in one fluid motion. "And you will be charged with assault if Ms. Chevalier decides to press charges." The officer looked at Rocky, who shook her head as she rubbed her neck.

"Lucky for you she is a forgiving woman," Jared said as he let Levine go.

"She poured hot coffee all over me, on purpose," Levine hissed.

Dad stood. "She tripped over that lip in the sidewalk, Edgar. It was a mistake."

Pickle walked up then. "The city owns this sidewalk, Levine. So if you want to claim they are negligent about a small lip between the sidewalk pavers, please do. It's a hard case to win, but I'll gladly take your money to help you try."

Levine glared at the two men and then back at Rocky. It looked like he wanted to say something, but with Jared there, I guess he thought better of it because he shot Rocky one more nasty look and then stormed off.

As soon as he was out of earshot, all of us cracked up. Then, Jared put on a very serious face and said, "Rocky, you know you cannot assault people with coffee, do you not?"

She frowned and hung her head. "Yes, Officer. I'm sorry, Officer."

Jared stepped closer, leaned over, and whispered, "That was brilliant."

"Thank you, sir," Rocky said, turning her fake show of

regret into a bow and then picked up the spilled coffee cups. "I'll be back with more coffee in a minute."

"I'll stand back," Dad said with a smile.

Jared and I took a donation of a whole bunch of dowel rods that Cate said would be perfect for artists and walked them over to the proper bin. "That was intense," I said.

"Yeah, Levine is a piece of work. He clearly just came by to make trouble," he said. "Glad I was here to intervene."

"Me, too . . . and I'm just glad you're here in general," I said as I kissed his cheek.

He blushed.

GIVEN how many coffee coupons we had given out and the number of customers I had seen go in the store, I decided it might be time for me to check in with Marcus. Of course, he was just fine when I asked him how things were going, and I could tell all was well in hand. But the store was quite full, so I decided to make the rounds.

I gathered up some abandoned coffee mugs and loaded some magazines and books into our library cart as I greeted customers and made book recommendations. A man in the self-help section asked if I could recommend anything that might help him change some negative thoughts, and after checking that he wasn't bothered by coarse language, I handed him a copy of *You Are a Bad A$$*. "So funny and so good," I said.

He smiled and took the book right to Marcus to buy it before drifting into the café as he read the first few pages. When he laughed out loud, I knew I'd made a good choice for him.

Before I knew it, eleven a.m. had rolled around, and Dad came to find me for the ceremony. We weren't doing anything fancy, just a chance for a few photos for social media and a quick announcement to let customers know what was happening. Mom had already issued a press release, so hopefully, the local paper would spread the word further.

Dad handed me a small pointed hammer and said quietly, "Your job is just to hammer at the mortar here," he pointed to a brick marked with a penciled x, "until the brick falls out. Nothing hard. Just a symbolic destruction."

I almost replied with a list of books that used destruction to symbolize psychological breakdown but decided that wasn't really a fitting discussion for this moment and simply took the hammer.

As I posed with the tool by the brick wall, a few camera flashes went off, and I could see Galen filming the whole thing too. Then Dad said, "Now, Harvey," with enough energy to make me feel like I was actually craning a wrecking ball into the bricks. That idea made me giggle because I was imagining Miley Cyrus's music video, and then I accidentally hit my own hand with the hammer because of my laughter.

Of course, the cameras caught that, and I could only try to keep smiling and swing again. This time, the tiniest shower of mortar poured loose followed by the brick, and Dad quickly stepped in and removed the tool from my hands. He hugged me, and we had our picture taken a few times together as I cradled the brick in front of us. And then it was over, and I breathed a sigh of relief.

I knew the store needed all the press it could get, and I was glad to see that a lot of the photographers went outside to get shots of the recycling event. But I hated that kind of attention. It was over, and I had a lot of good news coverage and a sympathy injury to my thumb to milk for the rest of the day.

As Dad was heading back outside to help Mom, he whispered, "Meet me behind the store in five. I have something to show you."

I looked at him with skepticism but said I'd be right out. My dad wasn't really a surprise kind of guy, but he was more excited than I'd seen him in a long time about this expansion project. As I walked to the back door, I wondered if he might like to help people with this sort of business project long-term. If so, my burgeoning desire to help women start businesses might just dovetail, pun intended, with his desire to oversee expansion projects.

I stepped out into the hot sun of the alley and let my eyes adjust to the bright light. I could smell the dumpster we used for the store and café reeking in the heat, and I was glad our usual pick up would be tomorrow, before the flies got really bad.

A quick scan showed that my dad hadn't made it back this way from the lot next door yet, so I spent a few minutes picking up the sort of litter that seems to just find its way to alleys. Soda cups, receipts, errant straws. I was just about to pick up one last plastic grocery bag when I noticed something red and glistening on the ground just by the corner of the store.

I bent over and looked more closely. I couldn't be sure, but that looked like blood, a little pool of blood. I quickly ran around the bulldozer into the lot and scanned for Dad. I didn't see him anywhere. My breath started to come more quickly the longer it took for me to find him.

At the front table, Mom was helping a man deliver some old cross-stitch supplies, but I interrupted their conversation. "Mom, where is Dad?"

She looked at me and said, "He was on his way to meet you a few minutes ago. You didn't see him?" The fear started to rise up into her face, and she quickly took the man's donation, handed him a coffee coupon, and stood up to help me as she said, "Elle, can you staff the table? We need to look for Burt."

Elle's brow furrowed in concern, but she didn't hesitate to move between her table and the donation one and manage both. Mom and I looked behind every box and then jogged into the store, where Jared was buying a soda from Rocky. "I was just coming to look—" he started.

"Dad is missing," I almost shouted. "I think I saw blood in the alley."

Jared put his soda down, took out his phone, and started to move toward the back while he made his call. "Tuck, Burt Beckett is missing. Come to the alley. I'll meet you there."

I let him take my hand as we walked as quickly as we could without causing alarm to the customers and burst out the back door. Dad still wasn't there. I raced over to the blood pool and showed Jared, who knelt and confirmed that it was indeed blood.

"Okay, we need to put out a BOLO." Jared was on his phone again as Tuck pulled his cruiser to a screeching stop just on the other side of the dumpster.

"Tell me what happened," Tuck said as he jogged over to us. I explained that Dad had wanted to meet me here to show me a surprise but that he hadn't been there when I came back and that I'd seen the blood when I was picking up trash.

"He left me about fifteen minutes ago to come talk to Harvey," Mom added. "Jared is putting out a BOLO."

"Good," Tuck said as he looked over his shoulder. "I've got a couple more temporary deputies coming over to help us look." He looked worn, and I couldn't help but think the last thing the sheriff needed was to have to supervise more officers as he geared up for the election in November. But today, I was really glad they were on hand.

"Sharon, I need to know what Burt was coming to talk to Harvey about," Tuck said.

Mom shot me a sad smile and said, "He was going to tell Harvey that he was starting his own nonprofit to help women business owners have financing and expertise for their businesses."

Tears sprung to my eyes. It was just what I'd been thinking

earlier. "Oh, Mom." I hugged her and let a sob rib through my chest. "I love that," I said into her shoulder before I forced myself to stop crying and stand up. "What now?" I said to the policemen.

"Who knew about this?" Tuck asked Mom.

"Just me, Walter . . . and Edgar Levine," she said with a gasp.

"What?! Why did Levine know?" Rage was pooling in my chest, and I had to take a few deep breaths to calm myself. Fortunately, Jared returned and put his arm around my waist, and my heartrate steadied a little.

"The land your father bought to build his office was another parcel owned by Levine." She pointed down the alley. "A little lot just at the end of the commercial district."

I sighed. "And he told Levine his plan?"

Mom nodded. "Levine wasn't willing to sell unless he was sure the land wouldn't be used for a business that might compete with his own." Mom swallowed hard. "He told your father he was happy to take his money for something so stupid."

I clenched my jaw and tried to take some more deep breaths, but the anger clawing at my chest was making that hard.

"What a bas—" Jared started to say.

"Okay, we need to see that lot," Tuck interrupted his deputy and gave him a little smile. "We can walk?"

"It's just a block away." She said over her shoulder as she marched in that direction.

Jared squeezed me and said, "I'll let everyone know and meet you there."

I nodded and jogged after Mom.

11

The lot Dad has purchased was adorable. A corner with trees on all sides and just enough room to build a long, narrow building in the middle. I could almost picture it. A little front porch with white trim against a beige office building. A table and chairs out front for casual meetings. A small kitchenette and bathroom at the back.

I stopped thinking about it, though, when I realized none of it would happen if we didn't find my dad. I felt my throat getting tighter but forced myself to take yet another deep breath as Jared jogged up to meet us. Simply the sight of him made me feel better.

"Everyone is on the lookout for your dad and Levine," he told me. "And the other officers are going to ask the people at the store and the event if they noticed anything."

"Good," Tuck said. "Harvey, Sharon, stay here. Jared, come with me." His tone was serious, and all of us did as we were told.

Mom and I watched as the two men walked across the small lot toward the far back corner where there stood, I could only now see, an ivy-covered shed. Mom and I grasped hands and squeezed all the blood from each other's fingers as we watched the men pry back the ivy and wrench open the metal door.

As they stepped inside, my knees started to buckle, but Mom wrapped an arm around my shoulders and held me up. "Whatever happens, Harvey, we can handle it," she whispered.

I tried to nod but found I was frozen with my eyes locked on the shed door. It seemed to take forever for the men to come back out, but when they did, they were both smiling. "He's not here," Jared shouted.

This time, Mom felt a little wobbly, so I braced her against me and said, "That's good news, Mom."

"It is," she said with a breathy wheeze, "but we still don't know where he is."

I cleared my throat and tried to sound confident. "We are going to find him," I said with far more assurance than I felt. "We are."

"Yes, we are," Jared said as he joined us on the sidewalk. "Listen, that wasn't a lot of blood back there. He's injured but not seriously, I don't think."

Tuck nodded. "Agreed. Let's head back to your store, Harvey, and regroup." He put his arm around Mom and led her up the sidewalk.

Jared took my hand and turned me to face him. "I'm here, Harvey. And we will find him." He held my gaze.

"Aren't police officers supposed to keep from making promises they aren't sure they can keep?" I asked with a small smile.

"Well, I intend to keep this one, and boyfriends make promises all the time." He blushed as he spoke.

I turned to follow Mom and Tuck. "Well, I like that," I said. "All of it. And thank you." I pulled his hand to my chest and held it tightly as we quickened our pace.

. . .

WHEN WE REACHED THE STORE, Elle was still ably staffing the tables with Stephen assisting, but none of our other friends were in sight. We hustled back into the store and saw all our friends gathered in the café and watching one of the deputies interview a white guy who looked to be in his twenties.

I let go of Jared's hand and sprinted over to the group. "What's going on?"

"This guy saw a black van pull up behind the store just about the time your dad went missing," Walter said. "He told me he saw someone hit your dad on the head with a bat and then drag him into the van."

It felt like someone had put a knife in my heart. "Someone kidnapped my dad," I whispered.

Jared pulled me close. "I'm going to go sit in on the interview," he told me. "Can you guys get Harvey and Sharon comfortable?"

Marcus took my hand and Mom's and led us over to the reading corner we'd just set up in the café. The next minute, Rocky was there with two steaming lattes and two blueberry scones. "Eat. You need your strength."

For a fleeting moment, I could see Rocky as a grandmother giving treats to her grandchildren, and the image made me smile. But then, I looked back over to the table where three police officers were talking to the only person who might be able to help us find my dad, and my heart dropped into my knees.

Fortunately, just as I thought I might break down completely, Cate pulled up a chair, took my hand in hers, and looked at my mom. "Burt is strong. So strong. He's going to be fine."

I felt two heavy hands rest on my shoulders. "He is. No doubt about it," Bear said from behind me.

As I watched Marcus continue to staff the store and deflect questions about what was going on in the café, I tried to think clearly. Dad was smart and physically quite strong, even for a man in his seventies. He would find a way out if we didn't find him first.

I tried to focus on the sweetness in the latte. I'd read a lot about mindfulness and food over the years, so I put that information to practice and thought about how the scone felt as it slid down my throat, about the warmth in the drink, about the way the mug felt in my hands. As I did, my breathing slowed, and I felt more calm. My thoughts were clearer, and my heart wasn't charging ahead anymore.

But then I realized, I needed to move. I knew I couldn't do anything more for my dad at the moment, but I was in my store. *My* store, and I could do something there.

I looked around at my friends, who were now loosely gathered around where Mom and I were sitting. "The police will tell us what we can do when they can. For now, will you all help me the way you were? Let's keep this event going and see if we can sell some books."

Mom smiled. "Good plan, Harvey, and one Burt would like since his new venture is inspired entirely by you, his brilliant, business-owning daughter."

I choked back more tears and stood up. "Let's do it."

Walter and Woody headed back outside to help Stephen and Elle; Cate and Lucas moved into the shop to tidy and fill in spaces on the front shelves and tables from the overstock; and Mom went to help Rocky tend the line at the café. I wandered into the children's section and hoped I might be able to distract myself by recommending some amazing books.

Fortunately, there was an adorable little boy with black curls sitting at a table with his mom. They were scanning a stack of picture books, and when I approached, he looked up at me and said, "Excuse me. I can only get one book. I can't decide."

I grinned. "I have the same problem all the time. Would you like a suggestion?"

He nodded, and I saw that he was missing one front tooth. The gap made him all the more adorable. "Let's see . . ." I said as I looked through the books on the table. "These are all great choices, but I think my favorite is this one." I held up a copy of *How To Catch A Dinosaur*. "It's really fun to read, and you get to find the dinosaur on every page."

"Okay!" the little man said definitively. "Let's get this one, Mama."

"Sounds good," she said and turned to me. "Thank you."

I smiled and watched them head to the register before putting the rest of their options back on the shelf. As I shelved, I noticed that, as was usual every few weeks, the picture books were terribly out of alphabetical order. So I began my routine of organizing them by the first letter of the author's last name and then reshelving them all. When I'd first opened the store, I'd tried just moving one book at a time, but I always had to restart when I did that because I ran out of room on some shelves and had too much on others. This way was more physical effort but took less time.

I was just reaching the Fs when Jared came and sat down on the floor beside me as I shelved. "You okay?" he asked.

I stopped and looked at him. "No, but I will be. This helps." I pointed at the stacks of books around me. "Gives me something to focus on instead of worrying."

He rubbed my back. "I have some good news. Our witness's description of the van included that the bumper was tied on with wire, and the van was just spotted over by the museum. Tuck and one of the other deputies are on their way over there now."

I stood up to grab my stack of G titles. "Okay," I said taking a long, deep breath. "But if they abandoned the van?"

"Right, he's probably not in there now," Jared said as he

picked up the other half of the books. "But we may find more to go on."

I nodded and continued shelving books. "Are you going over?" I asked, not sure what I wanted his answer to be.

"No, I'm staying here, with you." He flipped a stack of books in his hand and sifted them into alphabetical order. "We decided it was good to have a presence here."

I smiled. "Is that your only reason?" Even in the midst of this horrible moment, I couldn't help but flirt with this guy. I wasn't sure what that meant, but I didn't have the energy to figure it out the moment.

"Absolutely not," he said with a wink. "Now, are Hs next?" He handed me the stack he'd just sorted.

"You catch on quickly."

"Well, I know my alphabet, so that's a plus." He smiled and began sorting the next letter's worth of books.

We had made it through all the picture books and were just starting to check the Magic Tree House shelves to be sure they were in the right order when his phone rang. He stepped a few feet away from me to answer it. "Officer Watson."

I studied his face as he listened, but he was a textbook example of neutral expressions. He did nod a few times, and his eyes cut my way more than once. But in the entire approximately forty-five seconds he was on the phone, I had no idea what news he was getting, and I felt like I might pass out.

As I lowered myself into one of the tiny chairs nearby, Jared hung up and came right over. "As we expected, he wasn't there," he said as he settled into a chair next to me. "But we did find some mail that was pretty interesting." He studied my face. "Let's get you something to drink and we will talk about it with your mom, okay?"

I nodded and let him lead the way to the café where Mom and Cate were sitting and picking at a piece of banana nut bread. "Jared has news," I said as I pulled up another chair.

"A van fitting the description of the one that took Burt was found by the museum a bit ago. Burt wasn't inside, which is actually good news, but we did find some mail." He grabbed another chair and sat down. "Addressed to Burt."

Mom and I looked at each other. "Mail to my husband?" Mom said. "What did it say?"

"It looked like it was more of the prank he and Thomas were playing on each other." Jared leaned forward. "Tuck is on his way to talk with Thomas now. See if they can shed any more light on things."

I sat back in my chair and thought about this news. Thomas hadn't been around in a few days, but they traveled for work so I hadn't thought much about it. Now, though, I was suddenly suspicious. "Has Thomas been over to visit you all this week, Mom?"

Mom shook her head. "They were in Vancouver on business," she said absently. But then something sharpened in her eyes, and she looked at me. "Unless they weren't."

"When were they due back?" Jared asked Mom.

"Yesterday, I think. I'm not really sure though," she stared at her hands. "I should have been paying better attention."

Cate took her hands. "No, why would you pay attention to another person's travel schedule? This isn't your fault." She looked at me. "Or yours either."

I tried to believe her, but all I could feel was the rapid thudding of my heart in my chest.

Jared picked up his phone and tapped into the screen for a few minutes. "I've let Tuck know about Thomas's supposed travel plans." He looked at me and said, "Let's go see what people have brought in." He reached out his hand and helped me to my feet as Cate did the same for Mom.

I wasn't really interested in doing anything. My worry about Dad was just ratcheting up and up, and I wanted to be on my couch with my cat watching something totally mindless and engrossing, like *The Originals*. But the dogs needed a walk anyway, and I knew I wasn't going to go hide. So I leashed up Taco and Mayhem and followed Jared out the door.

As soon as we reached the table where Elle and Stephen were working, Stephen whipped around and took the dogs' leashes. "I've got this. Any favorite pee spots?" he asked with a grin.

"The entire world," I replied with a small smile. "Thanks."

"We've done well, Harvey. I sold out of flowers about a half hour ago, and most of the produce moved, too." She pointed at her nearly empty table. "And the co-op and Habitat are going to win out, too."

Walter walked over. "Plus, Woody did a little digging and found out where we could take old batteries and electronics since a bunch of folks had those to get rid of, too. So now we're keeping some ugly minerals out of the soil." He delivered this good news with a whole lot more enthusiasm than his usual, and I was grateful.

"Thanks so much, everyone. I'm sorry I've been so distracted," I said.

"Seriously," Cate snapped as she stepped in front of me. "Stop apologizing, Harvey. We have got this. Just look at that collection of building supplies. Someone actually dropped off several rolls of brand-new carpet and twenty two-by-fours."

I stared over at the massive collection of things in the lot and felt my heart lift a little. "That's amazing," I said. "And is all that furniture usable?"

"Every bit. Anything that was, um, icky," Lucas said with a laugh, "we put right into the dumpster. And before he left, your dad arranged to have the dumpster unloaded tonight over beside Woody's shop so he can do a big bonfire."

"But you'll be burning chemicals," Cate said. "Isn't that dangerous?"

Woody grinned. "I'm actually going to break everything

down, trash what shouldn't be burned, scrap the metal, and only burn what wood I can't use. You'd be surprised how much lumber is in an old sofa."

I shook my head. "You all have thought of everything." At that moment, a huge tractor trailer pulled up on the curb beside us, and I turned to see the Habitat logo on the side. "Wow, they're here early."

"We suggested they come early and start loading," Lucas said. "And I promised them tacos and cupcakes if they did."

I glanced over to where Lu's truck was parked on the other side of the street and felt my stomach gurgle. "I need some food," I said and took Mom's hand. "Come on. Let's get some mole."

Mom didn't resist, and the two of us walked across the street to get comfort food. Lu smiled at us as we stood beneath her window and then said, "I'm so sorry, Harvey and Sharon. But I know Burt's going to be okay." Then she handed down two plates, each with two chicken mole tacos on them before also passing us cups filled with something pink and fizzy. "Be my guinea pigs for my new drink? Watermelon soda. Let me know what you think?"

I took my debit card out of my back pocket and held it up.

"Are you kidding me? My taste testers do not pay," she said and smiled.

"Thank you," I said and then walked with Mom back to the tables by the lot. We moved to the side and watched as two strong men loaded door after window after sofa after stack of lumber into the trailer.

Even as they loaded, other people showed up with donations. Some of them went in other bins or the dumpster – no one wants a couch that smells like cigarette smoke Cate decided – but most things went right into the truck. It had been a wise idea for Walter to have them come early, and when the guys took a break to eat the tacos and lemon cupcakes Lucas gave them, they were smiling.

As Mom and I finished up our late lunch, Jared came from the back of the store with a small bag in his hands. "Does Burt chew bubble gum?" he asked as he held the bag with the pink blob up to us.

If I hadn't finished eating, I would have spit my food out in laughter. "Uh, no," I said. "My dad is strictly an Altoids man."

"That's right," Mom added. "He won't even do the cinnamon ones. Just the spearmint that burns the skin off your tongue." She smiled.

"Well, this was fresh and stuck to the wall right near the blood," Jared said. "Do *not* ask me how I know it was fresh."

"I won't. Don't worry," I said. "Maybe you should wash your hands."

"Already done," he said as he tugged a small bottle of hand sanitizer from his pocket. "Hazard of the job."

I grimaced, and then he smiled. "I'm kidding. I did use this, but I'm on my way in to wash for the entire alphabet long. Good thing I practiced it earlier today."

"You know all twenty-six letters. I can attest to that," I said and then dodged as he pretended to come at me with his gum hands. "Off with you," I chuckled.

Mom smiled at me. "You two are good together. You have fun."

I blushed. "I think so, too, but it's early days. We'll see what comes." I was downplaying the situation. I really liked this guy. Today, though, I couldn't think about that too much. My dad was missing, and that had to be my top priority.

I shifted my chair so it faced Mom more fully and said, "So, what do we know?"

She spun to mirror my position and answered immediately. "Someone had Thomas's letters in their possession when they kidnapped your father." She held up one finger and then added a second. "The person who took your father probably chewed bubble gum."

"Or one of the people did. The witness said someone grabbed Dad and pulled him into the van, but why would that person be out of the van if they were going to grab Dad?"

Mom nodded slowly. "Good point. So there were likely two people involved. One to talk to your father and distract him and one to grab him. Is that what you're thinking, too?"

"Exactly," I said as Jared grabbed a chair and slid it next to mine. "Can we tell you our theory?"

"Sure," he said and then listened as Mom told him what we'd just surmised.

"That's what Tuck and I think, too. Your father isn't exactly a small man, so it would likely take two people to pull him into the van unless one of them was," he looked over at the two Habitat staff people who were lifting yet another sofa like it was made only of foam, "like these guys."

I let my mind play over the suspect list that we'd written up on the murder board a few days earlier. "No one we thought might be involved fits that description unless Pickle's client is a female bodybuilder."

Mom glanced around. "Where is Pickle anyway?"

I stood and scanned the lot. "Not here. He was here this morning, though."

Jared frowned. "That weird? Was he supposed to be here all day?"

"As far as I knew. He didn't say differently." I could feel the pieces of this puzzle beginning to slide together in my mind, but I couldn't quite picture the image yet. "I'll text him."

"You okay?" I said in my text as I tried to sound nonchalant.

His reply was almost immediate. "I am. Just had a client emergency. Be back over if I can."

"Client emergency, he said." I looked from Mom and Jared,

and I could see the wheels turning in their heads, too. "Something's up."

"But he can't tell us anything about it," Jared said. "Sometimes the law is so frustrating." He shoved his fingers through his hair, and it flopped down into his face.

"But the lawmen aren't," I said as I pushed the hair off his forehead.

"I'll give you two a minute," Mom said. "I want to see what Bear has gotten for the co-op." She smiled at me, and when I looked at her, the weariness of worry was apparent on her face.

I turned back to Jared after she walked away. "We have to find him, Jared," I said.

He put his hands on both of my cheeks. "We will, Harvey. We will." Then he let his forehead drop gently against mine.

12

By the time we closed down the recycling event at five, the entire tractor trailer from Habitat was full to the brim and Woody had a full pickup load to take to the co-op. Cate and Lucas were loading up the museum's van with clothes for the local church thrift store, and Stephen and Walter were filling their sports car with electronics to take into Annapolis to recycle the next day.

Elle had made a killing on her flowers and had even booked a wedding while she worked. And from the number of pizzas Symeon sold and the amount of sweat on his brow from working the oven, I thought he and Max had done pretty well, too. When he told me that he'd waited until Mart's event was over to tell her about my dad and that she was on her way home, I thanked him for everything, including the exact right thing to do with my best friend, and gave him a big, sweaty hug.

The event had been a huge success, and when I coupled that with the small story about the store's expansion that made the local TV news at five, I knew I should be happy with a good day's work.

But my dad was still missing, and I couldn't get my mind

around why. My father as an astute business man, but he was also a tender-hearted guy who would never wrong anyone if he could help it.

Marcus and Rocky forced me to leave the store just after five, assuring me that everything was under control, that they'd call if they needed me, and that this was what they wanted to do to help me on this hard day. "You are good friends," I said as I leashed up the dogs and met Jared and Mom outside.

I couldn't bear the thought of Mom being alone and neither could she, so she walked with Jared and me back to my house, where we mixed a huge pitcher of margaritas with extra tequila. Tuck had told Jared he and Lu would be over in a bit and that he'd give us an update then, and while I was impatient for news, I realized that if Tuck had anything pressing to share, he wouldn't be coming over to keep us company or waiting to share it.

Jared, Mom, and I got settled into the backyard, the dogs with chewies and Jared gave me and mom margaritas. While Mom and I relaxed and tried to chatter about how many surplus couches there must be in St. Marin's, Jared lit the citronella torches that ringed the yard, set up a table he found in our guest room, and went inside, I presumed, to bring out the margarita pitcher.

Instead, he came back with an entourage that included Henri and Bear, Cate and Lucas, Elle, Stephen and Walter, Woody, and even Pickle, back from his client business. "You didn't think we were going to leave you to your own wild thoughts tonight did you?" Cate said as she unfolded a camping chair that she had carried in on her back. "What kind of friends would we be if we did that?"

"Pizza will be here in ten," Jared said, "and Lucas, I could use your hand with more margaritas."

Lucas stood and said, "You had me at tequila."

"But I didn't say tequi—" Jared said with a laugh. "Never

mind. Come on." He waved his arm, and Lucas trotted in with him.

As they slipped into the house, Aslan slipped out in a rare, feline backyard debut. We'd always offered her the chance to go outside when we were out here, but until now, she'd declined, preferring her diva-like lifestyle on the couch and beds. Tonight, though, she must have sensed I needed her because she came right to me, jumped up on my lap, and sniffed my margarita. She either wanted to comfort me or get lit. Maybe both. Whatever her reason, I was grateful when she curled up and went to sleep.

A knock at the back gate was followed by the appearance of Tuck and Lu with what appeared to be an entire tray of rice pudding. I smiled. Rice pudding was my favorite dessert, and Lu knew that. Somehow, she'd made it for me in the midst of her wildly busy afternoon, and I was so grateful.

Stephen and Walter pulled out the cornhole boards Mart and I had bought a few weeks earlier at a local farmers' market and paired us all, without our permission, into teams. Fortunately, Jared and I were a team, and so when he came back with the margaritas, I refilled my glass and then volunteered to have us go first.

It turns out my boyfriend is an ace at cornhole, and he sank every bag without even touching the edges. I, however, a margarita and a half plus a whole lot of stress into the evening was not as skilled. We ended up in a pretty solid draw with Walter and Stephen since Stephen was an ace and Walter, well, not.

Soon, Lu had set up the whiteboard from our kitchen against an empty chair and had become the Vanna White of cornhole score keepers. Between the tequila and the game, the mood was high in our backyard, and when Mart joined us, it got almost raucous for a bunch of middle-aged people. By which I mean, we laughed really loudly and got tipsy. No one did shots or anything. We weren't that far gone.

Despite the revelry brought on by our worry, I hadn't forgotten about Tuck's conversation with Thomas, and so when we all decided to sit down before we fell down, I asked Tuck if he minded sharing what he'd learned.

"Well, nothing, because I couldn't find them," he said. "I brought in three more deputies from Easton, and they are following up on every possible location Thomas could be. So far, no report." He held up the phone he was cradling in one hand opposite the iced tea he had in the other.

I looked over at Mom and tried to smile. But her face was mirroring my own worry. Our only clue had been Thomas, and now they were MIA. That didn't look good for them, but it looked even worse for my dad.

"We did, however, figure out whose van it was. It belongs to a man named Devon Springer," Tuck said. "He reported it stolen this morning." Tuck held Pickle's gaze for a moment and then looked away.

I looked from one man to the other. "What am I missing here?," I asked with exasperation.

Pickle shook his head. "I cannot say anything at all about this." He sighed and said, "I'm sorry."

"No, please don't," Tuck said. "We want you to be completely free of blame here, no matter what happens."

Pickle nodded.

Then Tuck turned to Mom and me. "Springer's girlfriend is Melinda, Pickle's client, and we suspect she and her boyfriend kidnapped your dad."

I bolted to my feet. "Well, why haven't you arrested them? Where are they? Where's my daddy?"

Jared stood and came over to me just as Mart moved to my other side.

Tuck continued. "We have their houses under surveillance.

So far, they're both at her place, and we haven't seen them leave. In a few minutes," Tuck checked the time on his phone, "an officer is going to deliver a package there and see if we can't get a peek in the house. I'll be on the line the whole time and will let you know as soon as we have more information." At this, he stood and went out the back gate, where I caught a glimpse of his cruiser.

Mart hugged me and then sat down, allowing Jared to pull me closer. "Do you want me to stay here with you?" he whispered. "Or do you want me to go with Tuck?"

I stared at him and smiled. "Thank you for asking. Please stay. Tuck has got this, and I need you."

The entire group of people around us let out a collective "aw" in delight, and I blushed from the bottom of my feet up through my scalp. But I didn't pull away from Jared's arms. They could all get blissed out if they wanted. I needed this comfort.

I didn't stay curled up on Jared very long, however, even though I wanted to. Too much PDA just wasn't my thing. Instead, I poured myself another margarita and sat back down. Fortunately, my friends were far better at small talk than I was, and they rehashed the day, discussed the strange things that people donated – "I had no idea the number of people who had liked lava lamps was so high." Walter said – and just generally kept the tone light while we waited for Tuck to come back.

After about as long as I could stand without going out and getting into the car with the sheriff, he came back through the gate. At the same moment, Mart's phone pinged, and she took it out of her pocket, read the screen, and then jumped up.

"They have Symeon," she shouted.

Tuck and Jared both stared at her and then moved to read her phone. "They got me out back. On our way to—" Jared read out loud.

"On our way to where?" Stephen shouted.

Mart paled. "That's all it says."

I felt my breath catch in my throat. Whoever had Dad had Symeon now too.

Both police officers moved to separate spots in the yard and began making phone calls. Cate took Mart by the hands and moved a chair in front of her, while Mom and I found each other and held on tight. This was getting scarier and scarier.

No one else talked, and I appreciated the silence. No amount of banter was going to make this situation less serious, but the quiet presence of my friends was buoying, and I knew they had me even if I didn't have myself.

Tuck ended his call and came over. "We have a lead. The officer who was watching the house saw both Devin and Polly leave about thirty minutes ago. They were driving an old pickup, and while the officer couldn't get close without being spotted, they did watch the truck go down the alley behind Main Street."

I heard Tuck's words and thankfully still had some quick reflexes because Mart lunged toward him just as I got an arm around her waist. "They watched them kidnap Symeon and didn't do anything!" The fear and anger in her voice spiked like icicles in the air.

"They didn't actually see them take him. If they had, they would have intervened. But given the text you just received, we suspect that's why the two were in the alley." He put a hand out and touched Mart's arm before she flinched away. "They are in pursuit, and Jared and I are going there now."

Jared was already halfway to the gate when he caught my eye, held my gaze, and nodded. Then, he and Tuck were off and into Tuck's cruiser.

It took both Stephen and I to keep Mart from jumping in her car and following them, but when she calmed down enough to hear us say that too much ruckus could tip the kidnappers off, she finally stopped fighting and dropped into a chair. "I can't have something happen to him, not Symeon."

I pulled her to me. "They're almost safe, Mart. Almost safe." I knew I was reassuring myself as much as I was calming her, but it didn't matter.

"Let's go inside," Cate said, and she and Walter began to clean up as Lucas blew out all the torches and got all three animals through the sliding glass door. Stephen led us inside and then brewed a pot of coffee and found the Kahlúa.

Soon, we all had coffee with a little extra as we sat around the living room. Someone had put *Glow Up* on the TV, and the sound of people creating beauty was a soft comfort in the room.

Still, the tension was thick, and it didn't seem like any of us knew what to do, except Lu, who got out her whiteboard and took bets on who would win the make-up competition none of us were really watching. Her enthusiastic egging us to bet more of the peach gummy rings Stephen dug out of the pantry was a nice distraction, and I found myself a tiny bit invested in whether Jack, Dolli, or Sophie would pull off the win.

Between the forced enthusiasm we all showed for a program that had zero impact on our lives, the mix of tequila and Kahlúa, and the steady presence of my friends, I was almost able to relax. Almost.

But when my phone and Mart's dinged at the same time, I nearly jumped out of the chair. It was Jared. The message was simple. "We found the truck, but not the men. Be there in fifteen."

As soon as I showed Mom the words, she started to cry, and since given that this was only the second time I'd ever seen her in tears, I couldn't hold back my own. The two of us huddled together on the couch and then pulled Mart closer when she joined us. We were a mess, and I didn't even care. All I could think about was how my dad was hurt and that he and Symeon were in some abandoned warehouse somewhere awful.

It didn't matter that this part of Maryland didn't really have lots of warehouses. I had seen too many kidnappings on TV to be reasonable at a time like this. I kept imagining rising waters or the red digital lights of a clock on a bomb. It was making me feel insane.

When Jared arrived, I knew I couldn't sit still any longer, and I asked Cate if she could be sure Mom and Mart had what they needed while I leashed up the dogs, grabbed Jared's hand, and started to walk. I had to move or I was going to pull my hair out, literally.

Fortunately, Jared didn't ask any questions but took the dogs and let me lead us up the road, around the corner, and toward the water. I had no plan for where we were going, so I just kept walking in whatever direction was available. Fortunately for us, there was a small gravel trail along the river, and the dogs took to the scents of whatever snakes or rabbits or skunks had come to the water in the past few hours, and so we had a beautiful view as the lights across the water came on and the fishers out for catfish began to turn on the strings of lights along their boats. If I hadn't been so worried, I might have found it soothing.

Instead, I barely lifted my head as we walked, and I just let the worst case scenarios spin round and round in my mind. Dad bleeding on the floor. Symeon tied up or drugged or unconscious. Some sort of danger in the building. It was a waking dream of horrors, and eventually, I realized I needed to pull out of it or I was going to be of no use to anyone, especially Dad and Symeon.

"Tell me about kidnappings," I said to Jared, who had been walking along silently this whole time.

He looked over at me briefly, pulled my hand tight against his side, and said, "Most of the time, they're just the result of someone being angry, and eventually, when the kidnapper calms down, the victims turn up." He smiled at me and kissed my fingers.

"And the rest of the time?" I looked at him with a faint hope that the answer was the victims weren't really victims but had just decided to drive across state lines to sample some world-renowned barbecues.

"We're not talking about the rest of the time, Harvey." He stopped me and turned me to face him so that I could see the lights on the water over his shoulder. "We are going to find them, Harvey. We are."

At that exact moment, Jared's phone pinged, and he read the message. "There's been a demand. We need to get back."

As if sensing the urgency, Taco and Mayhem took off at a run, and within moments, we were back in my living room to hear Tuck's news.

"The kidnappers have made a demand. They want all of us to hold a press conference at your store tomorrow, Harvey, to confess that we are gossips who have no respect for other people's feelings," Tuck said with a shake of his head. "Listen."

He put his phone on speaker and set it on the coffee table. The voice sounded like someone was talking through a kazoo. "The whole lot of you despicable people spread rumors, tell lies, and toss around stories about other people like they are yours to share. Tomorrow at nine a.m., you will either have every news station within a hundred miles at All Booked Up to confess your sin of gossip or you will never see these two betrayers again."

I half-expected my mom to stand up and protest, to say that we would do no such thing because it simply wasn't true. But while she looked so angry that her saliva had probably turned to venom, she didn't say a thing. No one did. We knew what we had to do.

After that, everyone headed home with promises to be at the store by eight a.m. and an assurance from Cate that she would let Marcus and Rocky know the situation this evening. Mart offered Mom her room and said she'd bunk with me, and Jared said he'd take the couch. Tuck said he had a deputy stationed outside the house and that he had given everyone instructions to go right home, lock up tight, and stay there until he or another officer in a marked car came to pick them up in the morning. "No one goes anywhere without an escort. Is that understood?" He looked pointedly at me.

"I got it, Tuck." I tried to smile as I closed and locked the door behind him, but I really just wanted to cry.

Instead, I went into the kitchen, made a giant bowl of popcorn, melted an entire stick of butter for it, and doused it in salt before sitting down, turning on *Ted Lasso* and snuggling up with Jared on one side and my mom on the other with Mart tucked next to her, all of us and a cat on the couch with two dogs at our feet. Eventually, Mom and Aslan headed off to bed, and I got Jared blankets and sheets for the couch before Mart and I climbed in, put our backs together, and cried ourselves to sleep.

THE NEXT MORNING, I woke far too early, at five-thirty, and decided I was going to try and do my usual routine of coffee and a book before making us all bacon and eggs for breakfast. But when I got up, Jared had already started the coffee pot, put on a skillet of bacon, and was rummaging in the fridge. "Help you find something?" I said.

"Cream cheese?" he said with a little blush.

"Oh, we buy it in bulk. You'll find it in the huge container with the blue lid on the second shelf." Mart and I both had a massive affinity for cream cheese, and I took a little pleasure that Jared gasped when he saw our stockpile.

"You are clearly the woman for me if you have this much

cream cheese on hand," he said and then put the container on the counter to come over and kiss me thoroughly.

I savored the kiss and then pulled back. "I haven't even brushed my teeth yet," I said.

"Who cares?" he said as he kissed me on the cheek and went back to his cooking. "You don't have any chives do you?"

"Out in the herb bed," I said as I pointed toward the front door.

"Perfect," he said as he grabbed the scissors from the knife block and headed out.

I decided I might as well go ahead with my plan, in a modified way, and picked up my latest read, *Who Moved My Goat Cheese?*, a really light and engaging cozy mystery – and sat down in my chair. This guy might as well know how much I love my morning ritual if he wanted to be a part of my life.

To his credit, when Jared came back in with a handful of chives and what looked like oregano, too, he took one look at me in my chair, smiled, and went and got me a cup of coffee. Then, he put on some quiet music and proceeded to finish cooking without saying a word.

I enjoyed another chapter of my book, sipped my coffee, and relished the understanding that this lovely man had for me, even as I breathed deeply to inhale the scent of bacon. When I heard him plating the food, I put my book aside, stood up, walked over, and hugged him from behind as I said, "Thank you."

"Are you kidding? I don't disturb people when they're reading. That's a cardinal sin for my mother. She taught me well." He turned around and hugged me to him. "Besides, it was lovely to see you relaxing, especially today."

As we sat and ate, I smiled and laughed, even forgetting that I was still in my Eeyore pajama pants and ratty old T-shirt. And when Mart and Mom joined us, each in their own pajamas, I suddenly felt my sense of home expand ten-fold. The morning was perfect . . . except for the fact that my father and Mart's boyfriend were being held hostage by some gossip-obsessed person.

With breakfast finished, the three of us women headed back to the bedrooms to shower and dress, and somehow, Mart found a bit of shaving cream and a brand new razor so Jared could clean up in the powder room up front.

I let Mart take the shower first, and while she did, I decided on black dress pants, a blue knit dress that I sometimes wore as a shirt, and my black sandals. I figured that would look professional but also nonchalant. I was willing to do anything to get my dad back, but the kidnappers didn't need to know that.

I was having one of those good hair days that meant it would be a mistake to actually wet this curly hair of mine. So I simply slipped on a thin blue headband, finger combed my curls, and got dressed before taking my turn to freshen up in the bathroom.

By the time we were ready to go at seven on the dot, we all looked a bit more done than our normal, even Mom in the clothes she'd worn yesterday because she had put her hair in a French twist and borrowed some of Mart's jewelry. Mart was in a short white dress with a chunky red necklace and red shoes, and Jared had put on his uniform that Tuck had dropped off to him last night, and he looked fresh and professional. And really handsome, too.

We all got into my car and drove to the shop, where Jared watched until we locked the door behind him and then went to do his portion of pick-ups of our friends. He and Tuck had a number of stops to make, and he wanted to be sure everyone was here in plenty of time to feel settled before the press showed up.

Mom, Mart, and I busied ourselves by tidying up and dusting the shelves that were practically dust-free anyway, and when Marcus, Rocky, and Lu knocked on the door a few minutes later, we all went to work prepping the café, stocking the shelves as full as possible, and staging the space for the press conference in the open floor near where the demolition was supposed to be beginning.

As the police cruisers started to drop off our friends in small groups, as if by silent agreement, everyone found a way to be busy. Henri washed the front windows of the store while Bear stocked the front register. Elle cleaned the bathrooms and even tidied the breakroom. Woody and Walter climbed the library ladder over and over again to get all of the backstock onto the floor so that the shelves would be as full as possible for the cameras.

By the time Pickle, Cate, and Lucas arrived with Tuck and Jared, the entire store was as clean as it had ever been, and I felt heartened by the morning's events – while still terrified.

At eight-forty-five, we started to see the press gathering outside. At least two news vans, several reporters with cameras, and even our friend Galen and his bulldog Mac were out on the sidewalk waiting. When Galen saw me, he waved and gave me a firm smile as if to say, "You've got this."

I swallowed hard, turned back to straighten the chairs we'd set up one more time, and then looked at my friends for a split second. The tears almost came then, so I gave them a crisp nod, walked to the door, and let the press in before retreating with everyone but Marcus and Rocky to the back room to do the final prep on the statements we'd been workshopping with each other.

At nine a.m. on the dot, we filed out and lined up in front of the cameras with the empty brick wall of the store behind us, and Mom began. "Thank you for coming today, everyone. As you may have heard, two of St. Marin's most wonderful men have been kidnapped, my husband and Symeon LeDel, the fine chef from Chez Cuisine just up the street."

"Apparently," she continued, "their kidnappers are under

the impression that those of us who stand before you have a problem with gossiping about our friends and neighbors. We did not perceive our actions as such, but we know that the impact of our words is far greater than our own self-perception, and for this, we apologize."

One by one, we each stepped forward and said the line we had memorized, "I am sorry for how my words have hurt people." And each of us had ourselves photographed from every angle as we stood there, the scrutiny of the entire community and beyond on us.

Then, given the fact that this was a press conference and there were expectations of such things, we took a few questions. Well, I took a few questions.

"Harvey, why do you think someone kidnapped your father and Symeon LeDel?" a reporter from the Annapolis TV station asked.

Tuck had coached me to be honest but cagey in my answers, so I said, "I don't know, but I hope they will return these men to us because my dad and Symeon are two of the kindest most generous people I know." I glanced back at Jared as I finished, and he nodded and smiled.

The questions got more intense after that though. Someone asked if the men were kidnapped because they were criminals, and another reporter implied they might be pedophiles. Despite my rising ire, I kept my cool and said, "These men are not criminals, and they would never, ever harm children. I have no idea why they were taken."

After I'd given some version of that same answer a few times, Galen raised his hand and said, "Is it true that your father was working on an addition to your bookstore when he was taken, Ms. Beckett?"

I swallowed hard and silently thanked Galen for his kind transition to something more simple and less painful. "Yes, that is true." I gestured to the wall behind me. "Demolition and construction were set to begin today, but as you can see, we have postponed work until Dad and Symeon are returned to us."

For a few moments, the questions focused on the store and our plans, and while I really just wanted all of this to be over, I knew I needed to appear open and kind, per Tuck's instructions, so I answered each query as briefly and clearly as I could. Finally, Tuck stepped forward and said, "As you can imagine, this is a very trying time for Ms. and Mrs. Beckett, so we will take only one more question."

A short, thin man with a large moustache and Clark Kent glasses raised his hand. I nodded at him and smiled. Then he said, "Did your father kill Margie Riordan?"

The blood drained from my face, and I felt like I might topple over backwards. But Tuck steadied my elbow with a slight touch and squeezed. "No, he did not," I said. "Thank you all for coming. Please help yourself to coffee in the café if you'd like."

I took Mom's hand and walked slowly toward the back room, and once the door closed, I collapsed into a chair and sobbed. Mom grabbed my hand, and the two of us sat, crying, for a few moments until the door opened behind us.

Mart came in, told us most of the reporters had left. "You did really well, Harvey," she said as she sat down and took my other hand. "That was brutal."

I nodded and took a hitching breath. "It was, but it's over, and maybe they'll let Symeon and Dad go now." I wanted to feel hopeful, but I didn't. It just didn't feel like this was over.

"Well, the good news," Mart said, "Is that something happened during the press conference that got Tuck and Jared moving. They rushed off as soon as it finished, so maybe they have a lead."

I sighed. "I hope so. I really hope so." There was nothing more I could do now, and I had a feeling that this morning's events were going to draw a whole bunch of looky-loos to the store. So I stood up, grabbed a napkin off the table to wipe my face, and said, "I'm going to work." As I headed toward the door, I turned back and said, "And get a latte and a cinnamon roll. Who's in?"

Both Mart and Mom stood and walked with me to the café. We were helpless, but we weren't hopeless, and good food and caffeine could carry us a long way today. Never one to be idle, Mom stepped behind the counter and helped Rocky with the small line that had already formed now that we'd officially opened for the day.

Marcus and I had decided we might as well let everyone in after the press conference was over, and it had been a good decision. The store and café were busy, and I was glad Mom had something to do while we waited for whatever came next.

When Mart and I reached the counter, Mom plated our rolls, and one for herself, and then said, "I'm going to work here for a bit. Let me know if Tuck or Jared comes in?"

"Of course," Mart said as she took her plate and handed me mine. "Thanks for the sustenance, Rocky."

"Anytime," she handed us each a giant mug and then smiled. "We've got this. Together."

I smiled. I could not imagine what I would have done if this had happened without my friends nearby. I would certainly not be able to stand upright or eat without them. That's for sure.

As I walked back into the shop, I looked around. Woody and Walter were actively working on the new addition, even if demolition wasn't going to move forward without my dad, at my request. They were sketching out shelf locations and staring at the wall with great interest. Stephen and Walter were chatting up the customers, suggesting items from the café, and generally lifting the mood. Cate and Lucas were straightening shelves as quickly as they were un-straightened, and while Elle staffed the register, Marcus was recommending books left and right. Meanwhile, Henri, Bear, and Pickle were bussing café tables like they weren't all highly paid professionals in their own fields.

Fortunately, the tourists were out in force on a mild August Sunday, and I lost myself in answering questions about books, running the register, and staying on top of the reshelves after everyone but the people who actually worked here went home, Cate and Lucas taking Mom with them. It was a busy day, and, normally, I would have been over the moon about our sales figures. But the fact that neither Jared or Tuck had been in touch since the press conference had me on edge.

So on edge, in fact, that when a snarky teenage girl giggled and pointed at me when she came in, I glared at her, suggested she check out the movie *Heathers* and do so somewhere other than my store. Fortunately, Marcus had a cooler head, told her that I was acting out the bookstore version of *Mean Girls* as a marketing ploy, and then suggested she and her friend follow him to find books that took place in a universe like that.

He did give me a disapproving look out as he walked by, and while I recognized I had been out of line, I found I couldn't feel sorry. I just didn't have it in me at the moment. That's when I knew it was time for me to head home, even if it was two hours earlier than I was scheduled to leave.

As soon as Marcus came back from helping the teenagers and telling me they "loved" how mean I'd seemed, with a roll of his eyes, I said, "I think I need to go home, eat something terrible for me, and pet my cat."

"Agreed," Marcus said as he gave me a hug. "I've got this, and I'll be in touch if anything strange happens, okay?"

I so hoped nothing strange would happen unless, of course, *strange* included my father walking through the front door. Otherwise, I needed to distract myself and be away from people who didn't know me lest I destroy my business in the process. I thanked Marcus, waved to Rocky, and then went out to the bench up the street with the dogs to wait for Mart to come get me. I really wanted to walk home alone, but I knew I'd be in all kinds of trouble with my friends if I did that, not to mention that I might be setting myself up to be kidnapped as well.

Besides, the sun was warm, the breeze was cool, and the street was busy. And when I sat down, I felt the heaviness in my bones that confirmed I had made the right decision. I needed to rest. Desperately needed to rest.

As I waited, I stretched my legs out on the sidewalk, put my head back on the seat, and closed my eyes. A few seconds later, I felt someone sit down next to me, and I started to lift my head to let Mart know I was ready to go when a hand tugged the hair at the back of my head just as a woman's voice said, "Don't move, and don't open your eyes."

13

I could feel my dogs resting against my feet, and while Taco was still prone, I could feel the rigidness of Mayhem's back against my leg. She knew something was wrong, but she also seemed to not feel like she could move. Instead, she trembled against my leg and let out a low growl.

"Oh no you don't, girl," the woman next to me said. "I'll be leaving shortly. You just hold steady."

Mayhem's body tightened further, and I knew that despite the warning, if this woman harmed me, she would lose a chunk of flesh in the process. But I didn't know what that would mean for Mayhem, so I tried to soothe my dog. "I'm alright, girl. Let's just see what this woman wants."

I nudged my foot a bit further under her and also slid my toes under Taco's head. Only then did I realized that the basset wasn't at all asleep but simply pretending to be so. He was as taut as Mayhem but choosing to act like he wasn't.

"You did well at the press conference this morning, Ms. Beckett. I almost believed you. But almost is not good enough, so I'm going to need you to take a little action. You know, put your money where your mouth is. Let your actions speak louder than your words."

I took a deep breath and tried to keep my voice steady, even as the grip on my hair tightened. "Is my father okay? Symeon? I need proof that they are alright before I agree to anything."

"Someone else has also watched all the episodes of *Ransom*, I see. It was such a shame the show didn't have more seasons. I could have used more tips. Seems like you could have, too. Maybe then you could have avoided your father and your friend's unfortunate circumstance." Her voice was light, as if she was talking about the menu choices at her favorite restaurant. "Keep your eyes closed and listen."

I could hear the sound of a phone ringing near my head, and then when someone answered, the woman said, "Let her hear them."

"This is Burt Beckett," my father said. "To whom am I speaking?"

I let out a small laugh. Even under duress, my father kept his formal grammar. "It's me, Dad. Are you okay?"

"Harvey?! We are fine. Are you okay? What is going on?"

The woman pulled the phone away as she said, "They are both fine. Now listen. I want you to destroy every magazine and every book in your shop that traffics in gossip. Celebrity memoirs, magazines, true crime books. Everything that includes someone telling stories that are not their own to tell. Burn them."

I nodded. "Okay, I can do that. Then, you will let my dad and Symeon go?"

The pressure on my hair lifted, and when I sat up and opened my eyes, the bench next to me was empty. I stood up and spun around, looking for the woman on the sidewalk around me. Her voice had been familiar, and I hoped that if I saw her I might recognize her. But as I scanned the faces moving away from me and even toward me on the sidewalk, I didn't get a pulse of familiarity at all.

Until Mart popped up next to me and said, "Ready?" She was smiling, but as she looked into my face, her expression grew dark. "What's wrong?"

I took out my phone and dialed Jared. "Someone just threatened me out here in broad daylight. I need you and Tuck now."

He said he'd be at the store right away, and when I looked toward the police station a second later, he was jogging up the sidewalk. The sight almost made me smile. Almost.

"Someone threatened you?" Mart shouted. "When?"

"Just now, while I was waiting for you." I didn't have the energy to replay the conversation more than once, so I asked her to help me get the dogs back inside the store.

She took another look at my face and then nodded before grabbing both leashes in her hand. "Let me help you up."

"I've got her," Jared said as he reached me, bent over, and took both my hands in his. "Are you okay?"

I stood up, and my knees shook. "I don't know," I said. "I need to get inside."

Jared wrapped an arm around me, met Mart's gaze, and then helped me follow her back up the street to my store. As we reached the door, a police siren sounded behind us, and Tuck jumped out of his cruiser, which he double-parked on the street.

"Harvey, are you—" he started to ask when Mart interrupted him.

"She needs to sit down," she said. "Now."

Apparently I looked as bad as I felt because Tuck stepped ahead of us, opened the door, and then quickly marched to Marcus at the register. The next minute, the two men were moving from customer to customer, and slowly the store emptied. We were clearly closing early, and I didn't even care.

As I sipped the tea Rocky had handed me and felt my heartrate return to normal, I tried to figure out why the woman had seemed familiar to me. She had talked about celebrity memoirs and true crime, so she clearly knew book genres. There was a cadence to her voice that rang a bell for me. I thought back over her words, and then the phrase, "Literary but with an edge" floated into my mind, and it hit me – she was the customer with the long blonde braid who had wanted the edgy literary fiction, the same woman who had asked Marcus about Margie's murder.

"I know who has my dad," I shouted.

Mart, who had sat with me as soon as I came back in, said, "What?! How, Harvey?"

"She's a customer. I can identify her." I was still shouting, and my anxiety was rising. It felt like one of those dreams where you know what you need to do or where you need to be but you're too late to get there or to finish on time, and yet you keep trying.

Jared was watching me carefully as he sat next to me in one of the café chairs. "Who is she, Harvey?" he asked quietly.

I shook my head. "I don't know her name, but if I see her, I'll recognize her. She was at the recycling thing here yesterday. I saw her. She's been into the store a couple of times."

Tuck pulled up a chair and sat down. "Okay, Harvey. We hear you. But first, tell us what happened to you."

Without thinking, I pulled my hands free from Mart's and headed toward the bookshelves. "There's not time. I need to do what she said before she hurts Dad or Symeon."

Mart followed after me and spun me toward her. "Harvey, you're not making sense. What about Symeon?"

"He's fine," I said as I pushed her hand off my arm. "But he won't be if we don't burn these books."

Marcus stepped in front of me and barred my path. Behind me, I felt someone else step close and saw Jared was right behind me. "Harvey, stop. You need to tell us what happened," Marcus said.

I started shaking my head frantically from side to side. "Don't you understand. She's going to kill them." I tried to dodge around Marcus, but he caught my shoulders squarely in my hands, and then I felt two arms wrap around me tight. "Let. Me. Go," I shouted.

"No, Harvey, I won't," Tuck said close to my ear. "You need to talk to us before you do something rash. Let us help you."

He turned me around, and I saw Mart, Jared, Rocky, and Marcus all standing around me, fear etched deep into their faces. Something about their concern cleared the fog of terror just enough that I was able to realize I wasn't thinking well.

I sank to the floor. "The woman, she let me talk to Dad." I sobbed then, and Jared sank to the floor beside me and pulled me close.

A FEW MINUTES and a shot of espresso later, I was seated back in the café with all my friends around me. I had explained what the woman on the bench had said about burning the books and magazines, told everyone again that I recognized her from the store, and confirmed that Dad and Symeon were both okay, for now.

As soon as I finished speaking, Tuck was on the phone to the deputies from Easton with a description of the woman I had seen and directions to follow her but not engage. "We don't want to cause her to act rashly," I heard him say.

"Harvey, I need to get out there and look, but Jared is going to stay with you," Tuck said and nodded at Jared. "You are not to leave his side. In fact, I don't want any of you to leave this store." He turned to Marcus. "Could you please call everyone else and ask them to come here, too? At this point, I think we need to keep everyone together and have an eye on you."

Marcus took out his phone.

"Remind them not to come alone either. Get someone to pick up Elle and Woody," Tuck said to Marcus, who nodded and kept texting.

As Tuck headed out, I knew I needed to let myself fall apart, but I wasn't about to do that out here in the open where all this started and that horrible woman might see me. I asked Jared if we could go to the back room for a minute.

He winked at me and said, "Sure thing, Beautiful." Then, he gently took my hand and led me back. When he closed the storeroom door behind him, he pulled me to him and let me sob against his chest for a few moments.

Once I'd had my release and been comforted a little, I forced myself to breathe, wiped my face with a tissue, and said, "Let's go find this woman."

Jared hugged me one more time. "Let's do it," he said as he held the storeroom door open for me and kissed my cheek as I walked by.

In the front of the store, our friends were beginning to gather. Elle and Woody had already arrived as had Mom, Lucas, and Cate. Everyone was in the café with mugs of coffee, and everyone looked strained and tired, just like I felt. "Hi," I said as I walked back in and hugged Mom, who was sitting with Cate. She looked more exhausted than I'd ever seen her, and while I had never doubted her love for my father, the look on her face told me far more about the depth of her feelings for him than any words ever could.

"You okay?" I asked her.

She huffed out a hard breath and said, "I am not, but I am." She smiled at me and said, "You?"

"Same." I looked over to the next table, where Mart and Elle were sitting, also hand in hand. "You mind?"

"No, go. We all need each other," Mom said.

I pulled my chair over to sit next to Mart, and her head fell against my shoulder. "Did you talk to him, Harvey?" she asked very quietly.

I sighed. "I didn't, but Dad said he was okay. My dad wouldn't lie about that, Mart. He's okay." I tilted my head to rest on hers and tried to breathe.

The bell above the front door sounded as Marcus opened it to let Henri, Bear, and Pickle in along with Stephen and Walter. A minute later, Lu knocked, and Marcus helped her carry a tray full of churros to Rocky's counter. I didn't feel much like eating but the smell of fried bread and cinnamon was comforting just the same.

"Do you think we should move away from the window?" Stephen asked. "She's probably watching."

I sat up and looked around and was about to suggest we move to the back of the store when Jared spoke. "Actually, Tuck and I think it's good you be up here. She needs to see you all together, and if you are up for it, Harvey, we think we need to act like we're gathering materials to burn, as she asked."

"You're buying time," Mom said with a flat voice. "You're trying to give Burt and Symeon more time."

Next to me, Mart let out a little whimper, and I pulled her close again. "They're okay," I whispered. "They're okay." I gave her a tight squeeze and then stood up. "Okay."

I looked into the faces of each of my friends and felt their compassion and support, and then, I slid my emotions aside and went into manager mode. "Elle and Mart, you two pull all the magazines with celebrity mentions. Stephen and Walter, true crime. Henri, Bear, celebrity memoir. Pickle, Mom, Marcus, and Rocky, let's scour the shelves for anything that has a hint of fact behind it that isn't about only the person writing it. We'll pull everything that might be mildly upsetting to this awful woman." My voice was firm, and I felt my resolve shore up behind it. I'd burn them if I had to.

"Give us an example of what you mean, Harvey?" Pickle said.

I thought for a minute. "Okay, *11/22/63* by Stephen King. It's fiction, but it takes place around the Kennedy assassination. Or *The Liar's Club* by Mary Karr – it's her memoir, but it deals with her mother's drinking."

Pickle nodded. "Maybe we should just get the memoirs, too, to be safe?"

I thought a minute and then agreed. "Let's take the books and magazines right to the front of the store. We'll pile them there like we don't care about them, but if you would, please take a surreptitious picture of the shelves before you remove titles. That way, we can get things back where they belong quickly."

Heads nodded around the room. "Rocky, can you help me move the front tables?" Marcus said. The two of them slid the two large display tables off to the side, and then we had a large open space on the floor, right by the front door. If she was watching, she was definitely going to see that.

Then, we dispersed to our corners and began pulling dozens and dozens of books off the shelves. Pickle and I headed to the memoirs, and while I loaded up his arms, I answered his questions about what the woman had said.

I carried my teetering stack to the front door, squatted down, and let the tower tumble from my arms. I winced as they fell over, but if this wasn't painful, then it wasn't what the kidnapper wanted. So I groaned and threw my hands over my head and then headed back to where Pickle waited for me to fill his arms.

"Tell me what this woman looks like, Harvey," Pickle said, and something about the way he asked gave me pause.

I studied his face, which was etched deep with lines and looked gray and drawn, and said, "She has a long, blonde braid. That's her most noticeable feature."

He shook his head and headed toward the front, mumbling something that sounded like, "But she's not blonde." When he came back, he asked, "Tell me more about her?"

Pickle grabbed the next section of books from the shelves and rotated them so they'd stack against my forearms. "She's small, maybe only five feet." I let my mind go back to our conversations about books and pictured the woman as we talked. "She moves like she's very fit, like maybe a dancer."

Pickle hissed. "And what else?"

I stared at him a moment and then said, "Her accent isn't Eastern Shore or even Southern, I don't think." But then I remembered how she'd said, "Homes" when we were talking about the author's work. "But maybe she is. Sometimes, she had those long o's and i's that I have even though most people don't think I sound Southern."

As Pickle put two more books on my arms, he sighed. "Yeah, I know just what you mean." He sat down then, right on the floor, and leaned back against the shelves. "Give me a minute, will you, Harvey? Maybe go help Stephen and Walter for a bit?"

I stared at him. His jaw was set and his gaze hard as he looked at the reference shelves across the aisle. So I left him and went to find Jared.

He and Rocky were scanning the poetry section for titles. It was a hard task because if you don't know the poems or the poet, it's difficult to know if the poems are about their lives. I quickly pulled *Bellocq's Ophelia* off the shelf and put it on their pile. I was just about to suggest we move over to cookbooks since I knew some them were commemorating historical events, like Hurricane Katrina, when Jared's phone rang.

"Yes. Okay. On my way. Send a deputy here?" he said.

"We think we got her, Harvey," he said as he moved toward the front door. "An anonymous tip just came in. Tuck and the other officers are on their way to a fishing cabin just outside of town. I'm meeting them there." He kissed me quickly and then sprinted toward his cruiser on the street.

I stared after him for a minute and then looked at Rocky, who was already walking away to tell the others the good news. I took a deep breath and went to find Pickle.

He was sitting right where I'd left him, still staring at the shelves in front of him. "You okay?" I asked.

He looked up at me and said, "I am now." Then he pushed himself to his feet and said, "Think Stephen has a flask on him."

"Does he ever not?" I said as I put my arm around his shoulder. "Let's go."

Fortunately, Stephen had come prepared, and we all shared generous portions of whiskey in the fresh cups of coffee that Rocky made for us as we waited for news in the café. I couldn't help the knot of grief I felt in my belly as I looked at the pile of books tumbling in the front of my store. I knew some of them were damaged, covers ripped, pages bent, but I also knew that we had needed to do this. We had needed this time, this moment, for many reasons. I glanced over at Pickle, but he avoided my eyes.

"Do we begin to reassemble?" Marcus said.

I felt my spirits lift just a little. "I think so. Can we all start to put the books back where we got them? You up for that?"

"Up for it. I can't wait," Cate said. "It nearly killed me to dump those books there. I can't imagine what it felt like for you, a real book lover."

"Worth it," was all I said as I headed to grab the pile of memoirs I had last contributed. As I began to stack the titles, I could see some damage on a few of them, so I said, "If you see a book that has been injured, let's make a triage pile." An idea was starting to form at the back of my mind, but I needed to let it build before I could act on it.

"Maybe you and Marcus should evaluate what's damaged while we put everything back?" Elle suggested.

"Good plan," I said as I moved toward the front of the pile and began sorting books by genre and condition. It was because I had my back to the front door that I didn't see it coming.

Something hard and heavy slammed into the back of my head, and I toppled forward onto the stack of books. The next minute, I heard the bell above the door sound, and then a foot was on the back of my neck.

"I told you to burn them," she said.

I tried to turn my head and look up, but she was pushing my face harder and harder into the books below me. The muscles in my neck were beginning to scream.

That's when I heard two snarls and then a yelp as Taco and Mayhem latched onto my attacker's leg and pulled.

The weight on my neck lifted, and I heard a thud behind me. When I looked over, I saw a tiny, brunette pinned beneath Marcus's arms and my two dogs growling with bared teeth as they stood guard on either side of me.

Stephen called the dogs off and petted them profusely as two sets of hands lifted me to my feet, and I looked over to see my mom, tears in her eyes. "Are you okay?"

I rubbed a hand over the back of my head and neck. I was going to be sore and swollen, but I wasn't bleeding, surprisingly. I nodded.

Then, I turned to see Bear and Walter help pull the woman to her feet. She strained against the men's arms, and while I could tell she was very strong, quite fit as I'd surmised, she was too small to wrench free from the two large men.

As she squirmed and struggled, she reminded me of a cat I'd once had who was so feral that if you tried to take her to the vet, she suddenly became super-cat with the strength of a thousand cats and the teeth of a shark. She hissed and tried to bite Walter, but the men held her fast.

Then, Pickle walked up. "Melinda?" The surprise in his voice was clear, and he didn't flinch when she tried to kick him. "Melinda, don't say anything. You hear me." His voice was firm, but she didn't seem to hear him.

"They only hear what they want to hear," she screamed. "They don't see the truth, only what makes for good gossip. They never see me."

I sighed and let myself feel a tiny bit of compassion for this woman who was so obviously very traumatized and very hurt. I almost wanted to hug her, but then I remembered what she had done to my father and Symeon, what she had just done to me. I stood and watched as the deputy Jared had sent ran in, took the woman, and handcuffed her arms behind her back before forcing her past the broken glass from the front door and out to the back seat of his cruiser.

Once she was contained, the officer came back in and began to interview us one by one. While he talked to Walter and Bear to see what they had witnessed, the rest of us milled around and waited.

Stephen looked at Pickle. "You knew her name," he said quietly.

"I do. She's my client."

14

For reasons we all understood, Pickle said absolutely nothing else about this woman Melinda. I was simply glad he had been there when she attacked me so that he could expose their relationship in a way that didn't implicate him.

But I didn't think much about that stuff then because I was still waiting to hear from Jared and Tuck about Dad and Symeon. And so were Mom and Mart. Mom was sitting quietly in a chair in the café with her forty-nine-millionth cup of tea from Rocky; Mart was pacing and intermittently shouting about whether this fishing cabin was actually a cabin in Evergreen, Colorado, or Shanghai; and I was alternating staring at my phone and staring out the window on the lookout for Jared's cruiser.

Finally, Stephen brought a chair over to the front window for me so I could sit with my dogs, who were completely unconscious. The excitement of earlier had drained them, and despite the fact that I was still a mess of anxiety, their adrenaline spikes had apparently already faded and left them completely exhausted. I kind of wanted to curl up on the dog bed with them and just rest, but I settled for petting their ears as they slept.

Henri and Bear had immediately cleaned up the glass, and Woody had salvaged a piece of plywood from the back of his truck to temporarily repair the front door. Marcus, Cate, and Rocky had managed to organize the books into categories and make a pile of those that suffered too much damage to be sold at full price, and I was able to say that I thought we could do a sidewalk sale next week, give people a discount on the damaged titles and still generate some income for those authors. Lucas had stripped the covers off of all the magazines since they were far too beaten up to be sold now, and I'd need to return them for a partial refund.

I could see that all this was happening, and I wanted to help, too. But between the pounding headache I had from being hit in the head with a brick – the one brick, ironically, we'd removed in the ceremony yesterday – and my ever-increasing worry, I was useless. So Walter and Stephen sat on the floor beside me and the dogs and kept me company. They didn't even try to talk to me, and I appreciated the quiet companionship more than I could say at the time.

I had just checked my phone for the eight-hundred-thirty-second time when a cruiser flew by the window, sirens blaring and lights on. All of us jumped up and ran to the front windows. My heart was squarely against my tonsils, and I was having a little trouble breathing. That was not a good sign, and I rushed over to grab Mom and hold her close.

At that moment, my phone dinged, and everyone rushed over as I opened Jared's message. "Your dad and Symeon are fine and with me. Tuck is in pursuit of the other suspect. Take everyone and go somewhere safe."

I read his words to myself and then out loud. "Where do we go?" Marcus asked.

"My house," Elle said. "It's remote, and most of you haven't been there."

Mom nodded. "Let's go."

Marcus ran to the back of the store and armed the alarm as everyone spilled out into the street. We left all the lights on just to deter anyone from trying to pry the plywood off the door, and then we sprinted toward the cars that were closest – mine and Stephen's. Everybody that is, except for Pickle. "I need to go to the station," he said as he hugged me before I got in my car. "I'll update you if I can." Then, he was off at a jog up the street.

It was a tight squeeze to get us all in two cars, but when Mart and Elle climbed into the hatch of my Subaru, we all fit and headed out with Elle driving my car and leading the way. Just to be safe and be sure that whoever Tuck was chasing hadn't double-backed and decided to follow us, she circled around town for a few loops before speeding up and shooting out toward her farm. As she reached her road, she slammed on the brakes and spun my car up the driveway with Stephen right behind. For a brief moment, I felt like I was in that car chase from *The Italian Job* but with an Outback and a Tesla instead of Minis. And with no one, apparently, chasing us.

As soon as we got to Elle's gorgeous house tucked into the hillside above her farm, we all jogged inside and proceeded to make sure all the doors and windows were locked. Taco and Mayhem made the rounds of the house to sniff and double-check the perimeter before collapsing on the deck that over-looked the farm below.

The deck was only accessible from the house, so as Elle, Stephen, and Walter prepped drinks and dinner, most of us found seats on the deck to look down at the bright colors and neat rows of Elle's flower and vegetable garden. This time of year, the zinnias and sunflowers were really putting on a show, and I let my gaze linger on the vibrancy of the blooms as they danced in the late afternoon breeze.

Mom and Mart sat near me, and after a few minutes of quiet, when the news about Dad and Symeon had sunk in and the frenzy of our race to Elle's house had subsided, Mom said, "He's okay."

I nodded, "And *he's* okay," I said to Mart.

Simultaneously, all of us took a deep breath, and then we laughed, good and long and hard. So long and hard, in fact, that Bear came over and checked on us. "You ladies all okay? Did someone slip you some laughing gas?"

Henri stepped up next to him. "Better," she said. "They're high on relief."

I nodded and stared out over the fields below again, and as I did, the cloud of dust behind an approaching car brought me to my feet. "Look," I said as I stepped toward the railing.

I didn't recognize the vehicle. A long, sleek sportscar of some sort, not a police cruiser for sure. But before I could say anything, Bear had his hand on my arm. "Inside. Now."

Without hesitation, I sprinted toward the door just behind Mart and Mom and the dogs at my heels. Everyone else followed suit, and as soon as we were all inside, we slammed the door shut and locked it, pulling the long curtains shut too.

Then, Walter and Stephen ran around the house to check all the doors and windows again just as Cate and Lucas shoved a heavy sideboard from Elle's front hallway against the door. "Which windows have ground access?" Woody asked Elle.

"Just the two in the back bedrooms and this one here," she said pointing toward the kitchen window above the sink. "I'll get this one."

Woody and Henri sprinted toward the further bedroom, and Mart, Lu, and I took the closer one as Bear followed behind us with a fireplace poker. I scanned the room and tugged a wooden baseball bat from the wall where Elle had it displayed. "Go be sure Woody and Henri have something," I said to Bear, and he bolted out of the room.

"We have crutches," Henri shouted to us, and then Mart grabbed a broom from behind the door and took up a position on the opposite side of the window from me.

That's when we heard the thundering of footsteps on the stairwell to the basement next to us. "The basement door," Stephen shouted through the wall.

"Bear," I screamed. "The basement."

The form of a large man tore past the bedroom door, and seconds later, we heard footsteps going down the stairs. The basement opened under the deck, and while we had been sure that all those doors and windows were locked, they were the easiest entry point into the house. I hoped the men were in time.

A moment later, though, I knew they hadn't made it because I heard a new voice, and it was taunting us from the stairwell. "It would be best if we could do this civilly, so maybe you will let me come up the stairs so that, well, your friend Stephen doesn't have to bleed."

I cringed and looked at Mart. "It's Thomas," I mouthed.

She nodded. We'd had dinner with Dad's friend a number of times, and their voice was very familiar. "Okay, we're coming into the living room," I said.

I quickly walked into the living room and slid the baseball bat under the front of the couch then watched Mart slip the broom against the doorframe. Henri was able to tuck her poker back by the fireplace just as first Walter then Bear and then Thomas with a pistol to Stephen's back emerged at the top of the stairs and moved into the living room.

A quick glance around the room told me everyone was here, well, almost everyone. Woody and Elle were still missing. I imagined Woody had stayed back in the bedroom, but where was Elle? And what were they thinking they could do with our friend held at gunpoint?

I couldn't worry about that, though, not with Stephen in

danger. "Thomas, what do you want? What happened?"

"Your father happened," they said with a sneer. "He talked me into that ridiculous game with the mail, and then that woman started telling everyone that I was dating your father. Then, he found out, and he left."

I sighed. "Who, Thomas? A man you were seeing?"

As Thomas nodded, the gun slipped a bit, and I saw Walter's head twitch at the motion. I had to keep him talking, buy us some time.

"He thought you and Dad were really dating?" I took a step closer, and when Thomas didn't move the gun back up, I took another. "He didn't believe you when you explained."

"Oh, he believed me, but he thought I was being cruel to play such a trick on that postmistress." Thomas shook his head. "He said that her gossiping was her problem, not mine, and I was no better than her to try to call her out on it."

I shook my head and tried to look really sympathetic as I took another step closer. "He should have taken your side, Thomas. You and Dad did us all a favor by exposing Margie's gossiping nature. She was the one who was wrong here."

Thomas waved the gun up in the air as they gestured with their hands. "That's what I said, but he wouldn't have any of it. And now he's gone, and the only person who has my back is Melinda . . . and you took her away, too." The gun was now directly pointed at my face. "You have all these friends, all the people who always support you. They'd never abandon you, even if they thought you made a mistake."

Mart stepped forward then, and Thomas swung the gun at her. "But we are your friends, Thomas. Everyone here loves you. We care about you."

A stricken look crossed over Thomas's face. "No, not like you care about Symeon or Burt. They are your people, and I wanted you to know what it felt like to lose them."

I studied Thomas's face and tried to figure out their logic.

Kidnapping Dad made sense, at least in the way Thomas was seeing things, but taking Symeon seemed random.

"Okay," I said, trying to draw his attention back to me. "What did Symeon do?"

"Are you kidding? He saw me that morning on his way to the post office, and he didn't even speak to me. Didn't even speak." They waved the gun around, and I saw movement in the hallway behind them. "I had just done the most horrific thing imaginable, and I'm sure I looked a fright. But he totally ignored me."

I glanced over at Mart who was staring at Thomas. I could see the rage tightening in her jaw, but she kept herself in check and said, "You're right. Being ignored always makes me upset, but that doesn't sound like Symeon. You're sure he saw you?"

"Of course he saw me," Thomas said as they leveled the gun at Mart again. "I was right there on the sidewalk across the street. He was almost to the post office, and I waved. But nothing. He didn't even look my way."

I sighed. "Thomas, I don't think he saw you." I spoke slowly. "I was sitting on the front stoop of the sidewalk with the girl who had just found Margie's body. I expect Symeon saw me before you waved and was just focused on getting to me. I don't think he meant to snub you at all."

A wave of fear washed over Thomas's face, and for a split second, the gun dropped to their side. At that moment, Jared leaped out of the hallway and tackled them, knocking the gun to the ground. Mart grabbed it and pointed it toward Thomas and, thus, at Jared. She was shaking so badly, I thought she might accidentally fire.

I stepped over to her and pushed her hands down so that the gun pointed at the floor. Then, Elle rushed up the stairs with Tuck right behind her. He came over, took the gun, and set it on the counter behind Mart and then helped Jared lift Thomas to his feet.

Then, Mart and I collapsed to the floor and lay there as the dogs licked our faces. Only when Jared came back in with Dad and Symeon did I move and only then just enough for Jared to lay down beside me and put my face in his neck.

WHEN I FINALLY PRIED MYSELF off Elle's hardwoods a few minutes later, Mom and Dad were tucked into each other in a corner of a couch, and Mart was on Symeon's lap in a chair on Elle's deck. Taco and Mayhem were sitting with Cate and Lucas at the dining room table, and everyone else was scattered about the room, except Tuck who had gone back to the station with Thomas in his cruiser. He had promised to come back shortly, once the prisoners were secured and he'd had a chance to talk with them.

Meanwhile, Walter and Elle set out the massive amount of pasta and the three sauces they had made earlier, and we all took plates but then mostly ignored the food and drank the wine that was also set out.

Jared took each of our statements separately in the front bedroom while the rest of us sat in a kind of stupefied silence, letting the alcohol and the quiet sunset outside soothe us. After I gave my statement to Jared, I had come back and put my head on Dad's lap on the couch. While I felt his breathing against me, he pulled his fingers through my curls again and again, just like he had done when I was little and we'd watch basketball games together on Sundays.

Eventually, Jared had all the information he needed, and he made himself a plate of food and proceeded to polish it off and go back for seconds as we all watched. When I raised one eyebrow at him, "A good day's work always gives me an appetite," he said as he sat down next to me and put one hand on my knee. "Especially when the people I care about are all okay."

I smiled and placed my hand over his. "So you knew it was Thomas when you got to the fishing cabin?"

Dad spoke, "It was Thomas's family place. I'd been there a couple times when we took their boat out. I told Tuck and Jared that as soon as they arrived."

"Plus, Thomas was the one who grabbed each of us after Melinda got our attention," Symeon added.

"I wanted to tell you on the phone, Harvey," Dad said.

I shook my head. "Nope, no guilt on your part. You didn't do this. Thomas and Melinda did. I was just glad to know you were both okay."

Mart kissed Symeon's cheek. "Same. Same," she said. "But how are Thomas and Melinda connected?"

"Ooh, ooh, I think I figured this one out," Cate said as she put her hand up higher and higher in the air like answering a question asked by her third-grade teacher. "They are siblings!"

Dad smiled but then shook his head. "Good try, Cate, but no. Anyone else want to venture a guess?"

Lucas side-eyed his wife and said, "They used to date."

"Ding. Ding. Ding," Symeon responded quietly. "Before Thomas came out, Melinda was their high school girlfriend. They stayed friends all this time."

Cate looked at her husband. "How did you know?"

"Rage like that only comes out when romantic love is involved," he said. When Cate raised an eyebrow at him, "What?! I read the Bridgerton books, you know."

I laughed.

"Wow, good on her," Henri said. "Well, until she was part of a kidnapping and assault scheme." A chuckle passed through the room.

"So she was just backing up Thomas's plan?" Mom asked with a look at Dad.

I shook my head. "I don't think so. Thomas sounded like

they were just all about revenge for being isolated, but when she threatened me it had to do with the gossip thing."

Stephen looked at Walter and then said, "When I was in high school, I dated a woman. She was wonderful and fun, and I really liked her . . . except I wasn't in love with her because, well . . ." He waved his hand in front of himself. "Years later, we saw each other at a high school reunion, and she told me that after we broke up, a lot of people said she had turned me gay and spread nasty rumors about her."

"And you think the same thing happened to Melinda?" Lu asked.

"I wouldn't be surprised," Walter said as he shrugged. "It happens a lot, unfortunately. Just part of our society's general ignorance and ugliness about queer identity."

My head dropped back on the couch. "I seriously do not understand why people have to hate other people."

Jared pulled me closer and said, "It's because you are incapable of hate."

Then, Symeon lifted Mart from his lap and got down on one knee in front of her. "I was going to try and do this at a more romantic spot, but I realize now I don't want to wait even one minute. Martha Weston, will you marry me?"

Mart gasped and then stared at him before nodding and then lunging to kiss him so quickly that he fell backward onto the floor.

"Thank goodness," Stephen said. "I was about to burst with the good news."

I stared at my friends and then I got it. "This was what you threatened Margie about?" I asked Symeon. "She knew you were going to propose."

As Symeon picked Mart up and snuggled her back into his lap, he said, "She opened my package with the ring I'd ordered." He looked at Mart. "It's at home. I'll get it on your finger right away."

Mart grinned. "You wanted to surprise me."

"Almost more than anything," he said.

The entire room cooed in delight, and Woody said, "On that note, I think I need to get on home. Can someone give me a lift to my truck?"

"I'll take you," Stephen said as he looked at Walter, "If you're ready." Walter nodded, and the three men stood.

"Mind giving us a ride home on the way?" Mom asked as she helped Dad to his feet.

"Not at all," Walter said. "You must be exhausted."

Dad nodded and then leaned down to give me a quick hug. "Thank you, Harvey."

I shook my head. "For what?"

Dad sighed. "Never mind. I'm too tired to explain how wonderful you are." He laughed and took Mom's hand.

Jared leaned over and whispered, "I'm not too tired. And if you'll let me, I'll keep helping you believe it, too."

A smile slid up my face and I let myself lean into this amazing man a bit further. "I think I can do that," I said, "but only after I sleep."

We were just about to head out with everyone else alongside when Tuck came in Elle's front door. Suddenly, I felt wide awake and sat back down, as did Lu, Cate, Lucas, Elle, and Jared.

"I'm just here to pick up my wife," Tuck said deadpan.

I groaned. "You do remember we're all voters and that you have an election coming up, right?"

"Well, when you put it like that," Tuck said with a smile as he sat down on the arm of Lu's chair. "Both Melinda and Thomas have confessed, and they have been officially charged with kidnapping and assault. Devon Springer was also arrested as co-conspirator. Thomas has, as you may have guessed, also been charged with murder."

I hadn't realized I was still tense until I felt the last of the burdens of the week falling away. "Did Melinda say what her motive was?"

"She honestly wasn't making a lot of sense. She just kept talking about how rumors hurt people and some things aren't anyone else's business. When she started chanting 'Sticks and Stones' over and over, I stopped listening." He rubbed his face. "Pickle is with her, and I expect he'll suggest she plea insanity, which is probably the right call."

"Can he still serve as her attorney even though he witnessed her attack Harvey?" Cate asked.

Tuck nodded. "Because he was her attorney before and because she is not trying to plead innocent, there's not conflict of interest on his part. He is only obligated to provide her the best defense he can."

"And if she pleads insanity . . ." Lucas didn't finish. It sounded like it was an easy case to make given what we'd seen and what Tuck had just described.

"Here's something I didn't know, though. She was at the press conference this morning," Tuck said and scanned our faces for our reactions.

I let my mind run back over the crowd that morning, but I had no recollection of anyone who looked like Melinda being there. "I didn't see her."

"Actually you did." He took out his phone and pulled up a photo and then zoomed in. "Right there."

"The dude with the moustache who asked about Margie's murder?" I stared at the photo another minute. "She's really good at costumes."

"For good reason. She does special effects make-up for a company over in Baltimore," Tuck said.

I stood up again. "Well, that's about the last revelation I can handle for the night. Who needs a ride?"

"Oh no," Jared said taking the keys from my hand. "I'll drive."

A crew is coming to repair your downstairs window tomorrow, Elle," Tuck said as he hugged her. "Until then, we've done a patch that should hold just fine overnight. They'll start here and then head to your store, Harvey. Meanwhile, we'll up patrols past here and the store for the night."

"Thanks, Tuck," Elle said as she held her front door open for me. "I may still sleep with the lights on tonight, anyway."

"Actually, if you have some lunch meat handy, I'll leave you two guard dogs to keep you company." Taco and Mayhem hadn't yet moved from their reclining poses by the couch, and I liked the idea of having them keep Elle company tonight. I knew how scary it was to sleep in your house the first night after someone invaded it.

"Really?" Elle said as she looked at the two hounds over her shoulder. "They do seem pretty comfortable."

"You think?" Tuck said.

"They are. Feed them whatever meat you have, give them some fresh water, and they'll be fine. If you really want comfort, let them in your bed," I said.

"Do I have to lift the big one?" she said with a glance at Taco.

"He's got surprisingly good ups," I said.

With that laugh, she closed the door, Tuck and Lu headed to his cruiser with Cate and Lucas while Jared, Mart, Symeon, and I all climbed into the Subaru for the ride back to our house.

Before we even got out of Elle's driveway, I was asleep, and when I woke to a gentle nudge on my shoulder, I found we were in our driveway, and Jared was pulling me up to stand so he could guide me into the house.

Mart and I found our pajamas from the night before and climbed into my bed after helping Jared set Symeon up with his spot on the couch. Jared took Mart's bed, and I think we were all asleep within minutes.

When I woke up the next morning, Mart was still drooling on the pillow beside me, but I could hear movement in the kitchen. I slid on my robe and wandered groggily into the sunlight, where two of the most attractive men I'd ever seen were cooking omelettes.

"Two days in a row, sir?" I said to Jared as I gave him a kiss on the cheek. "You're spoiling me."

"That's the plan," he said as he poured me a cup of coffee, added sweet creamer, and sprinkled the top with sugar. "That's the plan."

HARVEY AND MARCUS'S BOOK RECOMMENDATIONS

Here, you will find all the books that Harvey and Marcus recommend in *Epilogue To An Epitaph*. Don't pile them too high on your nightstand. :)

- *Once There Were Wolves* by Charlotte McConaghey
- *Women Who Run With Wolves* by Clarissa Pinkola Estes
- *A Wolf Called Wander* by Rosanne Parry and Monica Armino
- *Seven Days In June* by Tia Williams
- *The Omnivore's Dilemma* by Michael Pollan
- *Eating Animals* by Jonathan Safran Foer
- *The Mysterious Benedict Society* by Trenton Lee Stewart
- *Atomic Habits* by James Cleary
- *Beneath My Feet: Writers On Walking* edited by Duncan Minshull
- *Wanderlust* by Rebecca Solnit
- *This Savage Song* by Victoria Schwab
- *Music For Torching* by A. M. Homes

- *The Book of Accidents* by Chuck Wendig
- *Flowers in the Attic* by V. C. Andrews
- *Boomer Gets His Bounce Back: A Doc McStuffins Book* by Andrea Posner-Sanchez
- *Lolita* by Vladimir Nabokov
- *A Clockwork Orange* by Anthony Burgess
- *Winter's Bone* by Daniel Woodrell
- *Court Of Thorn and Roses* by Sarah J. Maas
- *You Are A Bad Ass* by Jen Sincero
- *How To Catch A Dinosaur* by Adam Wallace and Andy Elkerton
- *Bridgerton: The Duke And I* by Julia Quinn
- *11/22/63* by Stephen King
- *The Liar's Club* by Mary Karr

I have read all of these books and enjoyed them all for various reasons. I hope you may as well.

Happy Reading!

— ACF

WANT TO READ ABOUT HARVEY'S FIRST SLEUTHING EXPEDITION?

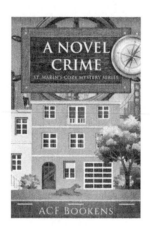

Join my Cozy Up email group for weekly book recs & a FREE copy of *A Novel Crime*, the prequel to the St. Marin's Cozy Mystery Series.
Sign-up here - https://bookens.andilit.com/CozyUp

ABOUT THE AUTHOR

ACF Bookens lives in the Blue Ridge Mountains of Virginia, where the mountain tops remind her that life is a rugged beauty of a beast worthy of our attention. When she's not writing, she enjoys chasing her son around the house with the full awareness she will never catch him, cross-stitching while she binge-watches police procedurals, and reading everything she can get her hands on. Find her at bookens.andilit.com.

f facebook.com/BookensCozyMysteries

ALSO BY ACF BOOKENS

St. Marin's Cozy Mystery Series

Publishable By Death

Entitled To Kill

Bound To Execute

Plotted For Murder

Tome To Tomb

Scripted To Slay

Proof Of Death

Epilogue of An Epitaph

Hardcover Homicide - Coming December 2021

Stitches In Crime Series

Crossed By Death

Bobbins and Bodies

Hanged By A Thread

Counted Corpse

Stitch X For Murder - Coming in November 2021

Sewn At The Crime - Coming in January 2022

Printed in Great Britain
by Amazon

82580386R00108